Enid Blyton®

NATURE STORIES

Look out for all of these enchanting story collections

by *Enid Blyton*

Animal Stories
Brer Rabbit
Cherry Tree Farm
Christmas Stories
Christmas Tales
Christmas Treats
Fireworks in Fairyland
Mr Galliano's Circus
Springtime Stories
Stories of Magic and Mischief
Stories of Wizards and Witches
Summer Adventure Stories
Summer Holiday Stories
Summertime Stories
Tales of Tricks and Treats
The Wizard's Umbrella
Winter Stories

Enid Blyton

NATURE STORIES

Hodder
Children's
Books

HODDER CHILDREN'S BOOKS

This collection first published in Great Britain in 2020
by Hodder & Stoughton

1 3 5 7 9 10 8 6 4 2

A CIP catalogue record for this book is available from the British Library.

ISBN 978 1 444 95423 4

Printed and bound in Great Britain by Clays Ltd, Elcograf S.p.A.

The paper and board used in this book are made from
wood from responsible sources.

Hodder Children's Books
An imprint of Hachette Children's Group
Part of Hodder & Stoughton
Carmelite House
50 Victoria Embankment
London EC4Y 0DZ

An Hachette UK Company
www.hachette.co.uk
www.hachettechildrens.co.uk

Contents

The Little Fawn   I

The Wonderful Carpet   15

Dozymouse and Flittermouse   27

The Poor Little Sparrow   39

The Sunset Fairies   51

The Grey Miner   63

The Pixies and the Primroses   75

How Derry the Dormouse Lost his Secret   81

The Blue Visitor   89

The Tail of Bup the Bunny   103

The Funny Little Hedgehog   113

Susan and the Birds   125

The Ugly Old Toad   137

Belinda and the Bulbs   149

Sly the Squirrel Gets a Shock   161

Lightwing the Swallow   171

The Elm Tree and the Willow   177

Black Bibs   183

Where Shall We Nest?   189

Betty and the Lambs' Tails   201

The Cross Little Tadpole   213

The Bumblebee Hums   225

Rabbity Ways   239

The Whistler   251

The Adventurers   265

The Crab with a Long Tail   277

The Little Ploughman   289

The Mistle Thrush and the Mistletoe 301

The Wonderful Traveller   313

New Tails for Old   327

Acknowledgements   339

The Little Fawn

The Little Fawn

FOR DAYS the sun had shone from a cloudless sky, and the oak leaves hung dry and dusty on the tree. The poppies flaunted their red frocks at the fieldside, throwing off their tight green caps in the early morning, and flinging down their red petals at night, as if they really were too hot to wear anything at all. Butterflies of all kinds came to the pink and white bramble flowers on the hedgerow, and wasps and bees hummed from dawn to dusk.

The hedgerow was thirsty. The grass beneath was parched and brown. Everything wanted the cool rain. The pond water fell lower and lower, and the fish began to be anxious. What would happen if they had no water to swim in? The moorhens talked of going to the big river, but they were fond of the little pond and stayed.

And then, late one afternoon the rain came. Great purple-black clouds sailed up from the south-west and covered all the sky. It seemed very dark after the brilliance of the summer sun. Then suddenly a flash of bright lightning tore the sky in half, and the startled birds flew to the hedge for shelter. Almost at once there came a loud peal of thunder that rolled around the sky, and sent the young rabbits scampering back to their burrows in fright.

And then, what a downpour! First came big drops that made wide round ripples on the pond, and set the oak-tree leaves dancing up and down. Then came a deluge of smaller drops, beating down faster and faster. The old toad crawled out from his stone and lay in the rainstorm, his mouth opening and shutting in delight as he felt the rain trickling down his back. Crowds of young frogs jumped out of the pond and hopped to the ditch for joy. The hedgehog found a sheltered place and curled up in disgust, for he didn't like the way the rain ran down his prickles. It tickled him.

Soon a delicious smell arose from the field and hedge – the smell of the rain sinking into the earth. All the animals sniffed it. It was good. In their ears sounded the rippling and gurgling, the splashing and the dripping of the rain. They heard every plant drinking greedily. They heard the excited moorhens scuttling in the rain over the pond. It was a glorious time.

The clouds grew blacker. The lightning flashed again and the thunder growled and grumbled like a great bear in the sky – and just as the storm was at its height there came the sound of tiny galloping hooves. They sounded through the pattering of the rain, and all the rabbits heard them and peeped out of their holes, the rain wetting their fine whiskers. The toad heard them too and crawled back quickly to his hole. He did not wish to be tramped on.

The newcomer ran to the hedgerow and stopped there in its shelter. It was a small fawn, a baby deer, only a few weeks old. The hedgerow was surprised, for it had never seen a fawn before.

The little fawn was trembling in all its limbs. Its soft eyes were wide with fright, and its tail swung to and fro. Another peal of thunder sounded overhead, beginning with a noise like a giant clapping of hands. The fawn closed its eyes in terror and sank down on the grass.

It was frightened of the storm. Its mother had left it safely hidden in the bracken of the distant wood, and had bade it stay there until she returned. But then the storm had come, and the little fawn, who had never seen lightning before, or heard thunder, had been terrified. The jays in the wood had screamed in delight at the rain, and the fawn had thought they were screeching in terror. Fear had filled his small beating heart and he had run from his hiding place, through the wood, across the fields – anywhere, anywhere, to get away from this dreadful noise and terrible flashing light.

But the storm seemed to follow him. The rain came and lashed him, beating into his eyes. The thunder rolled exactly above his head – or so it seemed to him. Where was his mother? Why did she not come to him? He was so frightened that his legs would no longer carry him and he sank down on the grass beside the old hedgerow.

He made a little bleating sound and the old mother rabbit, who had heard many young animals crying for their mother, looked out of a hole nearby. She saw the frightened fawn and was sorry for him. She ran out of her burrow in the rain and went up to the panting fawn.

'Don't be afraid,' she said. 'It is only a thunderstorm. It will pass. Be glad of the good rain, little creature, and lick it from the grass. It will taste good.'

The fawn looked at the soft-eyed rabbit and was comforted. It was good to see another creature near him, one that was not frightened. He put out his hot tongue and licked the wet grass. The raindrops were cool and sweet. He stopped trembling and lay calmly in the rain.

'Come under the hedgerow,' said the rabbit. 'You will get wet lying there. This hedgerow is thick and will shelter you well till the storm is past.'

The little fawn obediently pushed his way into the hedge and lay down in the dry, though he could easily reach the dripping grass with his pink tongue.

'Where do you come from?' asked the rabbit inquisitively. 'I have never seen you before, though I have heard my mother tell of creatures like you in the woods.'

'I am a young fallow deer,' said the fawn, looking at the rabbit out of his beautiful big eyes. 'I was born this summer. I live in the wood with my mother, and I have a fine hiding place there among the high bracken. There is no bracken here, or I would show you how well I can hide underneath the big green fronds.'

'Bracken is good for hiding in,' said the rabbit. 'Where are your antlers, little fawn? I thought deer had antlers growing out from their head.'

'I have none yet,' said the fawn. 'But next year they will begin to grow. They will look like two horns at first, but in the second year they will grow more like antlers and every year they will grow bigger and bigger, until I am full-grown and show great antlers such as I have seen on my father's head.'

'Surely those big antlers are a nuisance to you in the woods?' said the rabbit in surprise. 'Don't they catch in the tree branches as you run?'

'No,' said the fawn. 'We throw our heads backwards as we run, and then our antlers lie along our sides and do not catch in anything. Also they protect our bodies from any scratches or bruises we might get as we run through the trees and bushes. My mother has no antlers – but she had told me that I shall grow some soon.'

'Do you wear them all the year round?' asked the rabbit.

'Oh, no,' said the fawn. 'They drop off in the springtime and then grow again in a few weeks. On my head I have two little bumps, and it is from these I shall grow my antlers each year. My father has wonderful antlers, very large and spreading, and they show what a great age he is. But he will drop his antlers next springtime, and they will have to grow again from the knobs on his forehead. That is what my mother told me.'

'How strange!' said the rabbit in astonishment, looking at the little dappled fawn as he lay under the hedge. 'What do you eat, little creature?'

'Oh, I eat grass and toadstools and the shoots of young trees,' said the fawn, beginning to feel hungry. 'And often we eat the bark of trees. I should like something to eat now.'

'There are some turnips in the field on the other side of the hedge,' said the rabbit. 'Would you like some?'

The fawn did not know what turnips were, but he jumped to his feet and followed the rabbit, squeezing himself through the hedge. The storm was over now, but the rain still fell gently. The thunder was muttering far away over the hills, but there was no longer any lightning. Blue sky began to appear between the ragged clouds and once the sun peeped through.

All the hedgerow was hung with twinkling raindrops. The oak tree shone brilliantly, for every one of its leaves had been well washed by the rain. The fawn slipped into the turnip field and began to nibble at the young turnips. They were delicious.

When he had eaten enough he went back to the hedgerow. The rabbit followed him and told him that he should go back to the woods, for his mother would be anxious about him – and at that very moment the blackbird in the tree above sent out his alarm cry.

'*Kukka-kuk!* Beware! Here comes a strange enemy!'

Every animal scuttled back to its hole, and all the birds flew to the topmost branches. The little fawn stood up and smelt the air. Suddenly he made a strange, welcoming sound and rushed up to the newcomer. It was his mother, a big well-grown deer, with soft eyes and small, neat feet with cloven hooves.

She nuzzled her fawn in delight. She had missed him from his hiding place and had come to seek him.

'Come,' she said to him. 'You should not have run away, little fawn. Enemies might have seen you and captured you. You are safe under the bracken in the woods.'

'But a loud and flashing enemy came,' said the fawn, rubbing himself against his mother lovingly. 'I was afraid.'

'That was only a storm,' said his mother.

'There are good turnips in the field over there,' said the little fawn. 'I have eaten some.'

'We will stay under this hedge until the dark comes,' said the deer. 'Then we will feast on the turnips before we return to the woods. Let us find a dry place.'

Under the thick ivy was a big, dry patch, for the ivy leaves made a dense shelter there. The deer lay down with her fawn beside her and they waited until evening came. They lay so quiet that none of the hedgerow folk feared them, and little mice, the hedgehog and the toad went about their business just as usual.

After they had fed on the sweet turnips the little fawn called goodbye to the old rabbit who had been so kind, and then in the soft blue evening time the two trotted back to the woodlands.

'Come again!' called the rabbits, who liked the gentle deer. 'Come again and share our turnips!'

The Wonderful Carpet

The Wonderful Carpet

ONCE UPON a time there was a queen who loved beautiful things.

She paid a great deal of money for many lovely things in her palace. She went about looking for lovely chairs, and beautiful curtains, for well-carved chests, and splendid pictures. She hunted for gleaming glasses, and for shining candlesticks.

At last it seemed as if she could find no more things of beauty. There was nowhere else to look, no other shop to go to.

'Well, I will send out a notice to say that I will pay well for any lovely thing that is brought to me,' said the queen. 'Then maybe I shall get some wonderful treasures.'

So she sent out a notice.

'A large reward in gold will be paid to anyone who brings me something lovely.'

Then there came crowds of men and women, and even children, to her palace.

One man brought a necklace of carved green beads. Each one was carved in the shape of a flower.

But the queen was tired of necklaces. 'I already have one hundred and fifty different necklaces,' she told the man. 'I do not want any more.'

Another man brought a silken cushion, on which had been painted a peacock so lifelike that it really seemed to move.

But the queen did not like that either. 'I have too many cushions already,' she said. 'The peacock is nicely done, but I do not want another cushion.'

A woman brought a set of tiny animals, all carved out of black wood. They were perfect, and the queen could see every hair on the backs of the animals.

'I have animals carved in ivory that are as beautiful as these,' she said. 'I want no more.'

A child brought her a bubble pipe, and she blew her some bubbles. They bounced into the air from her pipe, and the queen saw that they were all the colours of the rainbow.

'See,' said the little girl, 'I have caught a rainbow in my bubbles. Would you not like to buy my pipe, Your Majesty, and then you could catch rainbows for yourself? It is a beautiful thing to do.'

'It is only a game for children,' said the queen. 'I have a bubble pipe that is made of glass so fine it looks like a bubble itself. I do not want your pipe, little girl.'

Day after day the queen saw beautiful things, and she wanted none of them. She grew tired of looking at them, and she even grew tired of looking at the lovely things that she herself had bought.

'I did not think I would ever get tired of loveliness,'

she said. 'Is there something the matter with me, that I can no longer find anything I think is beautiful enough to buy and keep?'

One day a little man came to see the queen. He had a sack on his back, which he put down when he bowed himself very low before her.

'Have you brought me something beautiful?' asked the queen. 'I hope it is not a chair, or beads, or something painted or carved. I am tired of those things.'

'I have brought you something so beautiful that no one has ever tired of it,' said the little man. He opened his sack, and shook out hundreds of little round things all over the floor. The queen stared at them in surprise.

'Do you call those beautiful?' she asked. 'I think they are ugly. This is a stupid joke, little man. I will put you in prison!'

'Your Majesty, these things I have brought you hold more beauty than any treasure you have in your great palace,' said the little man.

'More beauty than there is in that wonderful carpet you are standing on?' asked the queen.

The little man looked down at the marvellous carpet. He saw the beautiful pattern, and the glowing colours. He nodded his head.

'I bring you more beauty than there is in a hundred carpets like this,' he said.

'You could not bring me anything more beautiful than this carpet,' said the queen. 'Why, it cost three thousand pounds!'

'I bring you something that will make you a carpet for nothing,' said the little man. 'A carpet more beautiful than anything you have ever dreamt of. Your Majesty, you think that money can buy all the beauty there is. But I tell you that the most lovely things in the world cost nothing. And one of these I bring you.'

'Show me the beauty in it then,' said the queen, growing cross. 'I can see no beauty in these little brown things on my carpet.'

'Your Majesty, you know the wood that lies to the east of your palace?' said the little man. 'There are trees there, but little grows beneath them. Bury these things I have brought you, bury them in that wood, a few inches below the ground – and I promise you that when May time comes, you will have a carpet more beautiful than any you have ever seen!'

The queen was puzzled, and a little excited. Perhaps the little man was talking about a Magic Carpet. The queen had never bought anything magic. She hoped the little man's carpet would be enchanted, full of magic.

'I will do as you say,' she said. 'I will bury these little brown things in the ground, and I will wait until May time – then I will go to see this wonderful carpet you have promised me. But, little man, if I do not think it is wonderful, if I do not find it more beautiful than the carpet you are now standing on, I shall put you into prison for the rest of your life.'

'Your Majesty, if you do not tell me that the

beauty I bring you is worth more than all the treasures in your palace, then I will gladly spend the rest of my life in prison,' said the little man.

He went away. The queen called her servants, and gave them the queer little round things. 'Put them back into the sack, and take them to the bare wood that lies to the east of my palace,' she said. 'Bury them a few inches below the ground and leave them.'

The servants did what the queen commanded them. It was autumn then. The winter came later, with snow and frost. Then came the spring, and the queen remembered what the little man had told her.

It is April now, she thought to herself. *Soon it will be time to go and see this wonderful carpet that the little man promised me.*

Now, the little brown things that the man had brought to the queen were bluebell bulbs. When they were buried in the wood, they sent out small roots to hold themselves down firmly. They lay quietly there all the winter.

When the springtime came, the bulbs sent up long leaves that looked as if they had been folded in two, for there was a crease all the way down the middle. Then the sun shone warmly, and the spikes of flowers began to push up.

Up and up they grew, and one day hundreds of them began to open out into blue bells – bells that hung down the green stalk, looking as if they might ring at any moment!

The flowers were a most wonderful colour. More and more of them opened until the wood looked as if a carpet of shimmering, gleaming blue had been laid there. They swung gently in the wind, and sent out a delicious scent.

The queen came walking to the wood to see the carpet that the little man had promised her. She saw the sheets of bluebells in the distance, beautiful to see. She smelt their sweet scent. She saw how the flowers changed their colour as they swung a little in the wind and the sun.

'So this is the carpet!' she said. 'A carpet of bluebells! It looks like a blue lake, a blue, shimmering lake – and it is made of flowers!'

She stood and looked for a long, long time. Then she heard a voice, and she saw the little man standing beside her.

'Well, Your Majesty,' he said, 'do you not think I was right? Is not this carpet more beautiful than the one you have in your palace? It costs nothing – and it is a beauty that everyone can share. It is not put into a palace, and kept for a few to see.'

'Little man, you are right,' said the queen. 'I love beautiful things – but I have always thought that those I paid much gold for must be worth the most – but this carpet of bluebells is the loveliest thing I ever saw. Give me some more beauty like this, little man, and I shall be happier than I have ever been before!'

The little man was pleased. He took the queen to a nearby field, and showed her the golden sheets of buttercups, stretching as far as the eye could see.

He took her to the hills, and showed her the dancing cowslips, nodding their pretty heads in the wind. He took her to the lanes, and showed her where the hawthorn lay like drifting snow across the hedges.

'Lovely, lovely, lovely!' said the queen. 'Anyone can have my palace treasures now! These are more beautiful than anything I can buy. Oh, little man, tell everyone to find these things and be happy!'

Well, we will, won't we? We won't buy treasures and store them away for ourselves – but we will find buttercup fields and daisy banks, cowslip meadows and bluebell woods – and we will store them away in our minds so that we can always see them there whenever we want to!

Dozymouse and Flittermouse

Dozymouse and Flittermouse

THE LITTLE dormouse knew the hedgerow from end to end. He had lived there for two summers and winters, and he knew every creature that ran beneath the hedge, perched in the bushes, or flew in the air above. His big black eyes watched everything.

He was a small tawny-coloured mouse, with a long thickly furred tail. He could run and he could climb, and even the oak tree knew him well, for he had many times run up the trunk and along the branches to talk to the squirrel there.

At first the red squirrel had thought the dormouse was a tiny squirrel, for he had such a furry tail, such large, bright eyes, and the squirrel-like habit of sitting upright with a nut in his paws.

'A squirrel!' said the dormouse in surprise. 'No, not I! I'm one of the mouse family. I've lots of names – dormouse is my right name, but I'm often called Sleepymouse and sometimes Dozymouse. I sleep very soundly, you know.'

'Well, I know a queer creature called Flittermouse,' said the red squirrel. 'You must be a cousin of his.'

'I've never heard of him,' said the dormouse. 'Where does he live?'

'He lives inside the oak tree,' said the squirrel. 'Come and peep.'

The dormouse looked into the hollow trunk of the old oak tree. He saw something black there, hanging upside down, perfectly still.

'Why,' he said, 'it's a bat! I thought you said it was a flittermouse.'

'Well, so it is, isn't it?' said the squirrel. 'It's like a little brown mouse with big black wings that flit about in the dusk – a flittermouse.'

The dormouse woke up the bat. It stretched itself and unfolded its webby wings. It had hung itself up by its hook-like thumbs.

'Is it night-time?' asked the bat in a thin, squeaky voice. 'Are there many flies and beetles about?'

'It is indeed getting dark,' answered the dormouse. 'But, please tell me something. The squirrel says you must be a cousin of mine. But how can you be a mouse if you have wings? You must be a bird.'

'No, no,' said the bat, flying out of the tree and perching very awkwardly beside the dormouse. 'I am no bird. Look at me. I haven't a feather on my back. I don't lay eggs either.'

'What are your wings made of then?' asked the dormouse.

'Look!' said the bat, and he stretched out one of his strange wings. 'The bones of my fingers have grown enormously long, and I have grown black skin over them to make wings. Isn't it a good idea?'

'I wish *I* could do that,' said the dormouse. 'How do you grow your fingers so long?'

But he received no answer for the bat was off and away into the air, darting here and there easily and swiftly. He caught some evening beetles and popped each one into a little pouch he had by his tail. Then he feasted on them, giving high, little squeaks of delight as he flew.

The dormouse watched him in envy. He liked flies when he could catch them, though he found it better to feed on nuts or grain, for fly-food darted away, and nuts and grain kept still. He peeped inside the oak tree where the bat had hidden. It smelt strongly of bat.

'I'm glad I don't smell like that,' he said to himself, as he ran quickly down the tree. He stopped at the bottom, and sniffed in every direction. He was always on the lookout for weasels, who loved a feast of dormouse.

There was no enemy near, so the dormouse ran to his summer nest to tell his wife to come out and hunt.

He went to the hedgerow and clambered up the brambles. A little way up was his nest, in which he had had several families of tiny dormice that summer. Now the last of them had gone, and all were running about on their own. The dormouse sometimes met them in the hedgerow, but most of them had grown so big that he hardly knew them.

The nest was well made, tucked into the bramble stems. The dormouse had decided to make it of the bark from the stems of the old honeysuckle that grew further down the hedgerow. He had torn it off in long strips, and he and his wife had made their nest with the pieces. Inside they had lined the nest with leaves, so that it was cosy and warm. It was so well hidden that not even the rabbits guessed where it was.

In the daytime the dormice hid in their nest and slept soundly. At night they woke up and went hunting for food. They loved nuts, berries and grain, and if they chanced upon a fat caterpillar they would take that too. As the summer went by they grew fatter and fatter, and the nest shook with their weight!

'When the autumn comes we must build a nest underground,' said the dormice. 'This one will be too easily seen when the bramble leaves fall.'

When October came the dormice were so fat and round that there really was not enough room for them both in their nest. The nights became chilly. The dormice felt more and more sleepy.

So they hunted about and at last found a little tunnel going right down among the roots of the hedgerow, quite a long way underground. They took some moss down the hole and arranged it in a little round place among the roots. They would be warm and comfortable there, far away from any enemy.

'Now we must take plenty of food down to our new nest,' said the dormouse to his wife. 'We might wake up on a warm winter's day and feel hungry.'

It was while they were hunting for food that they heard the bat calling to them. The dormouse once again climbed the oak tree and looked at the queer little bat clinging clumsily to the branch.

'I want to say goodbye,' said the bat. 'It's getting cold now, and I am going to hide myself away for the winter.'

'We are just doing the same!' said the dormouse in surprise. 'We have made a nice nest far underground among the hedgerow roots, and we are hoarding up some food in case we wake up on a warm winter's day and want a meal.'

'I don't do that,' said the bat. 'My food wouldn't keep like yours. It would go bad, because I eat only beetles and flies. But if I wake up it will be such a warm spell that a few flies are sure to be about too, and I shall catch them. I am going to fly to an old cave I know across the fields. A great many of my relations will be there – big bats and little bats, long-eared bats and short-eared ones, and little common bats like myself.'

'Do you make a nest?' asked the dormouse.

'Of course not!' said the bat. 'No bat ever makes a

nest! We shall all hang ourselves up by our hooked thumbs, upside down, cover ourselves with our wings and soon we will be fast asleep.'

'What do you do with your young ones if you don't make a nest to keep them in?' asked the dormouse in surprise.

'Oh, we keep our little ones cuddled against our fur, even when we fly in the air,' answered the bat. 'They cling tightly and never fall. Well, dormouse, I hope I see you well and fat in the springtime. You look fat enough now!'

'So do you!' said the little dormouse.

'Ah, it's a good thing to get fat before the long, hungry wintertime!' said the bat. 'We shall get through the cold days comfortably then. Well, goodbye.'

'Just come and see my nest before you go,' begged the dormouse.

'I can't,' said the bat impatiently. 'Haven't you seen my knees? They turn backwards instead of forwards, so that I can't walk. I am only made for flying!' He rose into the air and darted swiftly away.

'Goodbye, little flittermouse!' called the dormouse, and then, feeling a touch of frost in the air, he ran quickly to his hole. His small, fat wife was waiting for him. Without a word they curled up together in the warm moss and fell asleep. They became as cold as ice, they seemed not to breathe, so soundly asleep were they – but a warm night would awaken them, and then they would feast eagerly on their little store of nuts in the roots of the hedgerow.

The Poor Little
Sparrow

The Poor Little Sparrow

EVERY MORNING James and Sylvia put out crumbs for the birds, and a little bowl of water. The birds always knew when the children were going to throw out the food, and they came flocking down to wait.

'Chirrup-chirrup!' said all the sparrows, dressed in brown.

'*Tirry-lee, tirry-lee!*' sang the robin in his creamy voice.

'Fizz, splutter, wheeee!' chattered the starlings in their funny voices.

'*Pink, pink!*' the pink-chested chaffinch shouted.

'Aren't they lovely?' said the children, as they threw

out the crumbs and some crusts from the toast. 'They really are friendly little things.'

The children knew all the birds, though it was difficult to tell one sparrow from another. They knew the smallest one of all, though, because he had one white feather in his tail, and that made him look rather odd.

One day the little sparrow flew down with the others, but it couldn't seem to stand on the ground properly. It fell over, then tried to stand upright again, and then fell over again.

'Look at the poor little sparrow,' said Sylvia, who was very tender-hearted. 'What's the matter with it? It can't stand.'

'It's hurt its leg,' said James. 'Oh, Sylvia, I believe its leg is broken. Can you see?'

Sylvia went slowly closer to the birds. They did not mind, for they trusted the two children. 'Oh, James, you are right,' she said. 'Its leg *is* broken. Whatever are we to do?'

Now that morning the poor little sparrow had been caught by a cat, but had managed to get away. Its little leg had been broken, and the tiny creature did not know why it could not stand properly, nor why it was in pain. It had joined the other birds as usual for its breakfast, but it could not eat for it felt too ill.

Suddenly it fell right over and lay on the grass. Its eyes closed. Sylvia picked it up gently and put its soft, little head against her cheek.

'Poor little sparrow,' she said. 'It says in the Bible that God sees every sparrow that falls, so I expect He saw you too, and hoped I would pick you up. Well, I have – but I don't know what to do to make you better.'

But her mother knew. As soon as she saw the little bird, she took out the old, empty canary's cage and put the sparrow on to some clean sand at the bottom of the cage.

'It has had a shock,' said their mother. 'It will come awake soon, and will be all right. Oh, look! Its leg is broken!'

'How can we mend it?' asked Sylvia, almost in tears.

'Well,' said her mother, 'if we break our legs the doctor sets the bone in the right position, and then ties it to something that will keep it straight till the broken bone joins together and grows properly again. What can we tie to the sparrow's tiny leg to keep it straight?'

'A match – a match!' cried James, and he emptied some out of a box.

'That's a good idea,' said Mother. She gently picked up the sparrow, whose eyes were still closed, and laid it on the table. Then she tried to set the poor little leg straight. With strands of silk she fastened the straight matchstick to the thin, small leg. It looked very strange – but now the broken leg was straight again.

'Oh, Mummy,' said Sylvia joyfully, 'you've done it so nicely. When the bone joins again, the leg will be quite all right, won't it?'

'I hope so,' said her mother, putting the sparrow into the cage and shutting the door. 'We shall keep the tiny thing in here, and feed it until the leg is quite right and then it shall go free again.'

When the sparrow opened its eyes it was surprised to find itself in a cage. Its leg still felt strange, but it now no longer fell over, because the matchstick supported it. The little bird flew to a perch and chirruped.

James gave it some seed. Sylvia gave it a mixture of potato and breadcrumbs, and the sparrow was simply delighted. It had a little dish of water for a bath and another dish to drink from, set at the side of the big cage. At first it fluttered its wings against the bars of the cage to get out, for it hated not being free. But, as it still did not feel very well, it soon gave up struggling and sat contentedly on a perch, feeding and bathing whenever it wanted to.

The leg healed quickly. It was marvellous to see it. The skin joined nicely, and the broken bone seemed to grow together at once.

'I think we might let our little sparrow fly away

now,' said their mother one day. 'I am sure his leg is all right.'

'Are you going to take the matchstick off now?' asked Sylvia.

'Yes,' said her mother. So she took hold of the half-frightened bird, and carefully and gently took away the silk binding from the leg and match. The match fell off – and the little leg was as straight and strong as ever.

'We've mended its leg! We've mended its leg!' shouted the children in delight. 'You aren't a poor little sparrow any more. Fly away, fly away!'

The sparrow gave a chirrup and flew straight out of the window. How glad it was to be out of the cage! It flew into the trees, and chirruped so loudly that all the other sparrows came round to hear what it had to say.

Now you would not think that a small sparrow could possibly help the children in anything, would you? And yet, a few weeks later, a very strange thing happened.

James and Sylvia had some glass marbles, the prettiest things you ever saw. They were blue and green and pink, and had white lines curving through them. James and Sylvia were very proud of them, for they had belonged to their father.

'You can't get marbles like these nowadays,' said Father. 'Take care of them.'

Well, James and Sylvia took them to play with in the fields, and there they met David, a big, rough boy whom none of the children liked. When he saw the marbles he came up.

'Give me those,' he said, 'and I'll give you some of mine.'

'No, thank you,' said James, gathering his marbles up quickly. But he wasn't quick enough. David grabbed some of them and ran off laughing. Sylvia and James went after him.

'They are our marbles!' shouted James. 'Give them back, David!'

'I'll put them somewhere and you take them,' called

back David – and what do you suppose he did with them? Why, the horrid boy dropped them all into a hole in a tree. Then he ran off, giggling.

James and Sylvia ran to the tree. They tried to slip their small hands into the hole but they couldn't. The hole was too small.

'We can't get our marbles out,' said Sylvia. 'They're gone. Oh, that horrid boy!'

'Chirrup!' said a cheerful little voice nearby. The children looked up. It was their little sparrow. They knew it was the same one because of the white feather in his tail.

'I wish you could get our marbles,' sighed James. 'Your foot is quite small enough to go into the hole, Sparrow.'

'Chirrup!' said the sparrow – and what do you think he did? Why, he flew to the hole, and instead of putting in his foot, he put the whole of himself in. Yes, he quite disappeared into that little hole – but not for long.

He popped up again, head first – and in his beak he held a green marble. He dropped it on to the ground and disappeared into the hole once more. Up he came, with a blue marble this time. The children were so astonished that they didn't even pick up the marbles.

The little sparrow fetched every single marble out of the hole before he flew off with a last cheerful chirrup. Then the children picked them up, and went racing home to tell their mother the strange and lovely happening.

'How very extraordinary!' she said. 'It must be put into a story, for everyone will love to read about the poor little sparrow that did such a kind thing. It just shows what friends we can make, if only we are kind to even the smallest things.'

So here is the story – and I do hope you enjoyed it.

The Sunset Fairies

The Sunset Fairies

THE SUNSET Fairies were very bored. For two whole weeks they hadn't had a single sunset to get ready.

'It's too bad of the weather clerk to keep sending these dull days!' grumbled Goldy. 'Those horrid clouds bank up the sky every evening, and there simply isn't a chance to paint a decent sunset!'

'It's the west wind that keeps sending all these clouds,' said Star Eyes. 'I asked the weather clerk about it yesterday. He says the west wind *won't* stop.'

'Well, I'm getting very bored,' yawned Little-Feet. 'I've a good mind to run away and do something exciting!'

'Listen! Here comes the weather clerk!' called Twinkle. 'Perhaps there's going to be a sunset tonight, after all!'

Just at that minute the weather clerk sailed up on an express cloud, and leant out to speak to the fairies.

'No sunset tonight,' he called. 'You can put your paints and brushes away, and go to bed.'

'Go to bed!' snorted Twinkle. 'Why, it's only four o'clock in the afternoon! I don't think much of *you*, Mr Weather Clerk! You can't even arrange a sunset once a week!'

The weather clerk drove off crossly, muttering something about the west wind being terribly obstinate these days.

'Well, I don't know what you others think,' said Little-Feet, putting her brushes and paints away neatly in a cloud cupboard, 'but *I* think it would be a fine chance today to go down and have some fun on the earth! We've got plenty of time, haven't we? It won't be dark till at least half past nine.'

All the others looked at each other.

'*Shall* we?' whispered one.

'*Could* we?' whispered another.

'*Let's!*' cried everybody at once, and stuffed their things away in a great hurry.

Then Little-Feet and the rest flew up to the travelling cloud, and sat down all over it.

'We want to go down to earth!' said Twinkle, settling herself comfortably. 'Down you go, little cloud, and rest on the top of that green hill.'

The cloud sank slowly down, and the excited fairies peered over the edge to see the earth gradually coming nearer.

When the cloud landed softly on the top of the grassy hill, all the fairies jumped off.

Twinkle tied the cloud to a buttercup and left it there.

'We'll come back here and find it again when we want to go back tonight,' she said. 'It will be quite safe there.'

Off they all went, hopping and skipping over the grasses and flying every now and then when they felt extra excited.

'Isn't it fun!' cried Little-Feet. 'Doesn't everything look different here!'

'It's very grey and dull,' said Goldy, pulling her pink frock closely round her. 'I miss the sunshine!'

'Oh, never mind that!' said Twinkle. 'You'll get plenty of it tomorrow.'

'Look, here's a pond!' cried Pinkie. 'Did you ever see such funny things as these flying about in the water?'

'They're fish,' said Twinkle scornfully, 'and they aren't flying; they're swimming. Those are fins, not wings.'

'Ha, ha!' laughed someone suddenly. 'Excuse me laughing, won't you – but whatever kind of fairies can you be not to know fish when you see them?'

The Sunset Fairies looked round in surprise. They saw a fine, fat rabbit sitting beneath a blackberry bush, washing his left ear vigorously.

'We're Sunset Fairies,' said Twinkle stiffly. 'We live in the clouds, and very few of us have ever been to earth before.'

'Oh, I see,' said the rabbit apologetically. 'Well, I can't say you've been giving us much in the way of sunsets lately!'

'No, we haven't,' sighed Little-Feet. 'But it's not *our* fault. Anyway we were so bored that we thought we'd come and have an adventure down here for a change.'

'How long can you stay?' asked the rabbit interestedly.

'Oh, till it's dark,' answered Twinkle. 'Why?'

'Well, the Mushroom Fairies have got a dance tonight,' explained the rabbit, beginning to wash his right ear. 'It starts at seven o'clock. Wouldn't you like to go?'

'A dance!' exclaimed all the Sunset Fairies at once. 'We've never been to a dance in our lives!'

'Dear me, is that so?' inquired the rabbit. 'Well,

then, I'm sure you'd enjoy this one. Wait here a minute, and I'll go and tell the Mushroom Fairies about you. If they've got enough for you to eat, I'm sure they'll be delighted to ask you.'

He scampered off in a mighty hurry. The fairies looked at one another excitedly.

'What an adventure!' said Pinkie. 'It's just our luck to happen on a dance night!'

They waited impatiently for the rabbit to come back. When he came, he carried a large yellow letter in his paw.

'Here you are,' he said, giving it to Twinkle.

Twinkle opened it. 'Please come to our dance tonight,' she read out. 'We would love to see you. Seven o'clock in the buttercup field. With love from the Mushroom Fairies.'

'Oh, how lovely!' they cried. 'We must wash and get ourselves ready.'

The rabbit kindly lent them a tiny tablet of soap and his best towel, and soon they were as busy as could be, washing their faces in the pond and doing their hair.

When the time came, the rabbit took them to the buttercup field, and introduced them to the Mushroom Fairies.

'We *are* so glad to meet you,' they cried, kissing the Sunset Fairies. 'You're just in time for the dance.'

Two grasshoppers, a beetle and a cricket began tuning up, and soon the merriest dance was being played.

There were cakes made of honey and pollen, and jellies made of cobweb dew and sugar, besides all kinds of wonderful sandwiches. The Sunset Fairies had never had such a good time in their lives.

Suddenly Twinkle looked up into the sky.

'Good gracious!' she cried. 'It's the moon shining up there! We must be terribly late. Come on, Sunset Fairies – say goodbye, and hurry to catch our cloud.'

Quickly the little pink fairies said goodbye and thank you, and hurried off to the top of the green hill.

But mercy me! Their cloud was gone! There was the buttercup they had tied it to – but no cloud at all!

'Oh dear, oh dear!' wept Goldy. 'Now we can't get back, for it's far too far for us to fly!'

Certainly there was no way of getting back! The fairies didn't know *what* to do. They began to shiver, for it was chilly and the dew was heavy on the grass.

'I wish we had our nice warm clouds to cuddle into,' said Star Eyes sadly.

'Let's ask the buttercups to take us into their buds,' said Twinkle.

But the buttercups wouldn't. 'We're too sleepy,' they said.

The fairies asked the poppies, but they wouldn't either, nor would the big marguerite daisies. They said it was too much bother to open.

The fairies got colder and colder, and Little-Feet began to sneeze. They huddled under a wild-rose bush and cuddled against each other. Then they heard a soft whispering voice.

'I'll take you into *my* buds,' said the wild-rose bush.

'You darling!' cried the fairies, and flew up into the bush to find the buds. Then they cuddled inside, let the petals curl over them, and fell fast asleep, as warm and as cosy as if they were inside a cloud.

They were awakened very early by an anxious voice.

'Sunset Fairies, Sunset Fairies, where are you? I want you to paint a sunrise for me!'

At once the fairies peeped out of the wild-rose buds – and there they saw the weather clerk, sitting in his express cloud, looking around *everywhere* for them!

They jumped out and ran to him gladly.

'Take us back,' they cried, 'we lost our cloud, and couldn't go back yesterday. We'd *love* to paint a sunrise for you.'

They clambered into the cloud, called goodbye to the wild-rose bush, and up they went to their work; and a very good job they made of it, even if they *were* ten minutes late.

But that isn't the end of the story – for when the wild-rose bush opened its buds they were the loveliest sunset pink imaginable, instead of white like all the other wild roses. The fairies had somehow left a bit of sunset behind them, and stained the petals a lovely pink.

So when you see a wild rose exactly the colour of a summer sunset, you'll know why – a sunset fairy has just been spending the night there!

The Grey Miner

The Grey Miner

THE HEDGEROW stood bare and cold in the November sunshine. The frost had stripped the last few leaves from the hawthorn, hazel and brambles, and only the ivy was green. The oak tree that spread its big branches overhead still had some rustling brown leaves left, and these shone like old copper in the sun.

The leaves from the hedgerow lay in dry heaps in the ditch below. They crackled when any creature trod on them. Their bright colours had faded to a dull brown; the little creatures of the hedgerow found them useful for nest-linings, for the dry leaves were cosy and warm to sleep in.

There were not many hedgerow folk about now. It was too cold. The dormice were fast asleep. The lizards and newts were hidden safely away, and the bat had hung himself upside down in a nearby cave. It was wintertime.

But there was one little creature who was still very busy on this sunshiny November day. He did not go to sleep for the winter as some of the hedgerow creatures did, because he was always too hungry to sleep for long. He was a little grey mole, the miner of the hedgerow.

He lived so much underground that his eyes were almost no use to him; they had become so deeply buried in his velvety fur. But he had little use for eyes – it was his nose and his ears that helped him to find his food!

All through the summer days he had hunted for worms, grubs, slugs and beetles. He had gone down the underground runs that had been used by hundreds of moles before – long, straight runs worn smooth and round by the passing of many velvety bodies. From these runs the mole had tunnelled sideways in search of worms, throwing up the earth as he went, making many little molehills that showed the way he had gone.

Now that the winter had come there were fewer creatures about, and sometimes many days passed before the mole met anyone on his journeys, except little grey miners like himself. Today he was frightened, for a strange thing had happened. He had had a nest deep in a molehill on the other side of the field, not far from a little brook. For four days the rain had fallen without stopping, and at the end of the fourth day the brook had overflowed its banks. The water had flooded the mole's tunnel and had poured into his nest.

In a great fright, the little creature began to tunnel upwards, and at last came up into the open air on the very top of his molehill. Water was all around him –

only the height of his hill saved him from the flood.

Soon the water went down a little, and the mole stepped into it. He did not dare to tunnel downwards, for he was afraid of being caught by the water below ground. He found that the water round his hill was deep, but he could swim well so away he went, striking out with his spade-like front paws as fast as he could.

Soon he came to the end of the water. He was on the earth again. He burrowed downwards, throwing out the soil with his paws, and at last struck a tunnel, one of the many that ran across the field. He went along it and reached the hedgerow, which he knew quite well. There was a fine straight run that ran all along the hedgerow. It was dry and felt warm. The mole made up his mind to make a new nest under the hedge, so he began to make a side tunnel towards the hedgerow.

His sharp nose smelt a worm as he worked. At once he thrust his strong snout into the earth and dug swiftly with his clawed feet. In a trice he reached the worm, which lay coiled up cosily in its small chamber of earth, and he gobbled it up greedily. Then he went on with his tunnelling.

Now just nearby was a fine hold used by a hedgehog for her winter sleep. She lay curled up there, dry and warm. When the back wall of her hole gave way and the mole appeared behind her, the hedgehog woke up in a fright. She at once thought it was an enemy, and curled herself up all the more tightly.

'Move yourself,' said the mole, pushing up against the frightened hedgehog. He had a high, squeaky voice like a bat. 'I am tunnelling here.'

The hedgehog knew the mole's voice, and uncurled at once.

'Why do you disturb me?' she asked angrily. 'I was fast asleep. You should sleep too in this cold weather.'

'I wish I could,' said the mole. 'But I am always too hungry. Do you know whether there are many grubs about under this hedgerow? I should like to find some of those fat grey leatherjackets; they make a fine meal, and I am very hungry.'

The hedgehog looked at the mole's velvety coat, so different from her own mass of spines.

'You will find plenty of worms and grubs in this bank,' she said. 'Tell me, how do you manage to keep your coat so clean and tidy, living underground as you do, tunnelling all day long?'

'It's easy,' said the mole. 'My coat is very short and all the hairs stand straight up – they do not lie backwards like the rabbit's. So it doesn't really matter if I go forwards or backwards in my tunnels – the hairs will bend either way quite easily. Why don't you tunnel too? You have a long snout, like mine, and could easily burrow with it.'

'No, I couldn't,' said the hedgehog. 'I use it for turning over leaves when I look for slugs, but it isn't strong like yours. I have seen you thrusting your snout into the earth and throwing it up easily. May I see your paws? I have often wanted to see how it is you can dig so well.'

The mole held out a front hand. It was very curious,

for the palm was turned outwards, instead of inwards. It was very broad, and the nails were large and strong. The mole could not close his hand; he always had to hold it open. It was immensely strong, exactly the right shape for digging and tunnelling.

'I shall have my nest under this hedgerow,' said the mole. 'It seems a good place. I can smell plenty of worms about.'

'How do you build your nest?' asked the hedgehog sleepily. 'I just find a hole and line it with leaves and moss.'

'Oh, I shall tunnel until I am right under the hedge,' answered the mole. 'Then I shall make a nice hole there, throwing up the earth above it till there is quite a big hill. I expect I shall have to make one or two tunnels through the hill to throw out all the earth. If I feel cold I shall line my hole with a few leaves, as you have done. It will be my resting place, and when I am not there I shall be hunting all around under the ground for grubs and worms.'

'Don't eat them all,' begged the hedgehog. 'I might go hunting myself on a warm winter's night.'

'Tell me when you do, and I'll take you to the best hunting ground,' promised the mole.

'Will you have any children living with you in your nest?' asked the hedgehog, remembering how she had had seven little hedgehogs with her in the summertime.

'Oh, no,' said the mole. 'I never have them in *my* nest. I had a wife who made a very big nest for our young ones this summer. It was out in the middle of the field, though I warned her it was not a good place. She took leaves and grasses to her hole in her mouth, to make the nest nice and soft. I saw the young moles. They were queer, wrinkled little creatures. But before they could look after themselves a dog came and smelt them out. He destroyed the nest hill and found the little ones. My wife escaped down the tunnel, but she was so frightened that she fled to another field.'

'A badger ate one of *my* little ones,' said the

hedgehog, suddenly remembering her poor youngster. 'But all the rest are grown up and have found holes of their own to sleep in. I don't think I should know them now if I met them. You had better go now, mole. I want to sleep again.'

The hedgehog curled herself up tightly and in a few minutes was snoring softly. The mole turned and went back into his tunnel. He dug hard for a few minutes, ate three worms and a grub, and then found himself just underneath the thickest part of the hedgerow, where he planned to make his nest.

He began to loosen the earth with his strong spade-like paws. He pushed it upwards with his snout. As the hole became big, so the hill above grew big too, for all the earth from the hole was thrown there. Soon the mole had to take the earth right up through the hill, and to do that he had to tunnel up it. But it was not long before he had the inner hole big enough to satisfy himself. He settled down in it comfortably to have a short sleep, for he was tired.

His hill rose up under the brambles in the hedgerow and was well hidden.

He fell asleep and dreamt of all the things he liked so much to eat. The rabbits came out from their hole and looked at the new mound of earth in the hedgerow.

'A mole has come to live here,' they said. 'We shall sometimes meet him where his tunnels cross our burrows. Our hedgerow will shelter yet one more creature this winter!'

The oak tree rustled loudly. It would feel yet another patter of feet over its deep and tangled roots, and it was glad.

The Pixies and the Primroses

The Pixies and the Primroses

ONCE UPON a time the fairy king complained that primroses were too pale a yellow.

'They are such pretty flowers,' he said. 'It is a shame to make them look so pale and washed out. I would like them to be as yellow as the daffodils. The daffodils are beautiful with their deep yellow trumpets.'

'Your Majesty,' said Scatterbrain the pixie, bowing low. 'Will you let me have the job of painting all the primroses a lovely deep yellow? I and my friends can do this easily. I have a special sunshine paint that will be just the colour!'

'I don't know if I can trust you to do a job like that,' said the king doubtfully, looking at the little pixie. 'You know how forgetful you are, Scatterbrain. Why, only this morning you forgot to put any sugar on my porridge, and when I told you about it you shook the salt cellar over the plate! If I let you do this job, you would probably paint the primroses sky blue or something silly like that.'

'Your Majesty, you hurt me very much when you talk like that,' said Scatterbrain, going very red. 'All I have to do is to give out the paint to my friends, and by the morning the job will be done! Every primrose in the woods will be finished! You will be delighted!'

'Very well,' said the king. 'You may do the work, Scatterbrain – but do be careful!'

Scatterbrain was overjoyed. He called all his pixie friends and told them of the work the king had given them. 'Come to me tonight and I will give you each a pot of yellow paint,' said the little pixie.

So that night all the pixies went to Scatterbrain's

house. He had been mixing his yellow paint that day, and had a big pot of it. He poured some into hundreds of small pots, and gave one to each pixie, with a nice new brush. Off they all ran to the woods.

I haven't done anything silly this *time*, thought Scatterbrain, as he emptied the last lot of paint into a tiny pot for himself. 'Won't the king be pleased in the morning when he sees the primroses as yellow as daffodils!'

The pixies set to work. They began in the middle of each primrose and painted very carefully. The deep yellow colour looked lovely.

They went on painting – and then they began to look rather alarmed. Their paint pots were very tiny and only held a little paint. By the time they had painted all round the centre of the primroses there was no more paint left in anyone's pot.

And so, by the time the morning came, the king went to walk in the wood to see what sort of job Scatterbrain had made of the primroses. He found that each of them had a pretty deep yellow centre – but that was all!

'Your Majesty, I didn't give the pixies enough paint,' said Scatterbrain, ashamed. 'Let me make some more and finish the primroses.'

'Certainly not,' said the king. 'You would only make another muddle of some kind! The primroses are quite pretty with a deep yellow bit in the middle. Leave them as they are!'

So they were left. You can still see the little bit of deep yellow paint in the centre of each one.

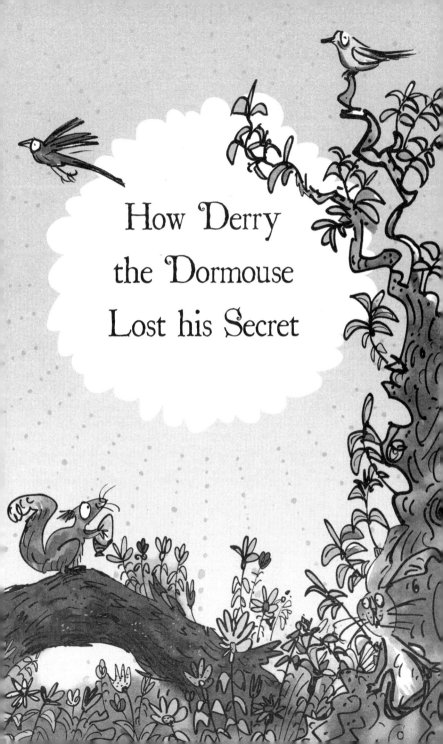

How Derry
the Dormouse
Lost his Secret

How Derry the Dormouse Lost his Secret

ONCE UPON a time Derry the dormouse hid a nice little store of cherry stones in the hole of a hollow tree. He was so pleased with them that he went to look at them every day. Sometimes he nibbled one, and when he came to the kernel inside he ate it all up.

But he couldn't keep his secret to himself. When he met Bright-Eyes the squirrel, he called to him, 'Bend your head down, Bright-Eyes, and I will tell you something. I have a store of cherry stones in the hollow tree! It is nice to have a secret like that!'

Bright-Eyes listened, and then leapt up the trunk of a tree. At the top he found Screech the jay, looking very colourful in the sun.

'Bend your head down, Screech, and I will tell you something,' he said. 'Someone has a store of cherry stones in the hollow tree. There is a secret for you if you like!'

Screech opened his beak and made a noise like his name. Then he flew off and came down in a field where Four-Paws the hare was nibbling grass.

'Bend your head down, Four-Paws, and I will tell you something,' said Screech. 'Someone has a store of cherry stones in the hollow tree. There is a secret for you if you like!'

Four-Paws listened eagerly and then went bounding over the field. It wasn't long before he met Mowdie the mole.

'Bend your head down, Mowdie, and I will tell you something,' he said. 'Someone has a store of cherry stones in the hollow tree. There is a secret for you if you like!'

Mowdie listened and then ran off in a hurry. Soon

she saw Grunt the hedgehog, and she spoke to him.

'Bend your head down, Grunt, and I will tell you something,' she said. 'Someone has a store of cherry stones in the hollow tree. There is a secret for you if you like!'

Grunt listened, and then went on his way down the ditch. Soon he met Flicker the robin, and he called to him.

'Bend your head down, Flicker, and I will tell you something,' he said. 'Someone has a store of cherry stones in the hollow tree. There is a secret for you if you like!'

Flicker listened and flew off. When he saw Fuff-Fuff the long-tailed field mouse, he called to him.

'Bend your head down, Fuff-Fuff, and I will tell you something,' said Flicker. 'Someone has a store of cherry stones in the hollow tree. There is a secret for you if you like!'

Fuff-Fuff listened and ran off. He went straight to the hollow tree, and there he found the store of cherry stones. Then, quickly and quietly, he carried them one by one in his mouth to where he had his home in a hole in the bank of the field.

That evening Screech, Four-Paws, Mowdie, Grunt and Flicker all met together with Derry, and with one accord they began to tell him his secret.

'Oh, Derry,' they said. 'We have a secret to tell you. Someone has a store of cherry stones in the hollow tree.'

'Why, that is *my* secret!' said Derry the dormouse in surprise. 'How is it you all know it? But, since you do know it, come and I will show you my store of cherry stones in the hollow tree.'

He took them to the tree, and they all peered in. Alas and alack, the hole was empty! No cherry stones were to be seen at all.

'Oh! Oh!' wept Derry the dormouse. 'Now my secret is gone. My cherry stones are stolen. If I had only kept my secret, I should have kept my stones too! Where, oh where, is my little store of cherry stones that I gathered so carefully from the orchard down the valley?'

But no one knew. Only Fuff-Fuff could have told him, and Fuff-Fuff wasn't going to. He was sitting in his hole, nibbling through the cherry stones to get at the kernels inside. Oh, naughty little Fuff-Fuff!

The Blue Visitor

The Blue Visitor

THE POND that lay quietly near the hedgerow was always a very busy place. The frogs croaked there, and newts swam about in the water. Wild ducks sometimes came, and the slow-flying heron, with his deep voice calling, '*Kronk! Kronk!*' Snakes hunted for fish in the water, swimming gracefully, and most of the birds drank from the edge. So did the hedgerow animals – some in the daytime, but most of them at night.

King of the pond was the little black moorhen, with his bobbing, red-marked head and long dark-green legs. He lived there all the year round, feeding on fish, tadpoles, water weeds and anything else he could pick up for a living. He could often be heard clucking among the reeds, and the hedgerow folk knew him very well indeed. He could run as fast as he could swim, and sometimes he spread his wings and flew off to the farm away in the distance to have a meal of grain.

The year before he had had a nice little wife, but she had been caught by a cunning fox. So when the springtime came and the moorhen wanted a nest, there was no little mate to help him to build one.

'Where shall I find a mate?' he said to himself as he swam across the pond, bobbing his perky little head. 'The primroses are here, the sky is as blue as the little speedwell on the bank, it is springtime – but I have no one to love!'

That day a visitor came to the pond. It was a kingfisher, gleaming blue and green in the sunshine. He was rather a stumpy bird to look at, with a long, strong beak, and a short tail – but his brightly coloured feathers made him beautiful! His chestnut breast shone, his back was sky blue, and his head and wings gleamed a marvellous green as he turned here and there. The moorhen gaped at him in envy. *He* was black, sober black, with the front of his head and base of his bill a bright red – a dull creature compared with the brilliance of the kingfisher!

The kingfisher was friendly. He sat on an alder branch that stretched over the pond and looked for fish in the water below.

'You will find more fish if you come down and swim on the water,' said the moorhen. 'That is how I catch *my* fish!'

'And this is how I catch *mine*!' called the kingfisher, diving into the water like an arrow. He came up with a fish wriggling in his mouth. He knocked it sharply against the alder branch and killed it. Then he swallowed it, head first.

'Very clever,' said the moorhen admiringly. 'I wish I could do that.'

'Do you happen to know of a good hole in the bank

of this pond where I could nest?' asked the kingfisher. 'This seems to be a fine pond for fish. It would be a good place to bring up my young ones. I have a beautiful little wife and we are looking for a place to nest in.'

'Yes!' said the moorhen eagerly. 'There is a fine hole in the bank over by the hedgerow there, at the end of the pond. It once belonged to a water vole. Would that do, do you think?'

The kingfisher flew down to the hole and went inside. He soon came out, excited and pleased.

'Just the thing!' he cried. 'I shall fetch my wife and bring her to live here. I am so glad I visited this pond today!'

'Do you know of a little moorhen who would like to come and live with me and build a nest?' called the moorhen.

'I'll see!' said the kingfisher, and off he flew. The next day he was back again with his wife, who was just as brilliant as he was. How excited she was to see the hole in the bank! It did not go quite far enough in, so the two birds busily dug it further back until they had made a tunnel quite three feet long. It sloped upwards a little to prevent the rain from running in. The moorhen went to see the hole, and the kingfisher told him that he was going to make a nest at the end of it.

'I forgot to tell you something,' he said. 'I saw a moorhen yesterday on the river and she would like to come and live with you. She will soon be here.'

The moorhen was very much excited to hear this. He preened his wings and made them glossy. He swam all round the pond crying, 'I shall soon have a wife!' Then he looked carefully for a good place in which to nest.

The little moorhen came the next day. She was a timid little thing, but pretty and good-natured. The moorhen was delighted. He showed her all round the pond and she thought it very comfortable and well stocked with food.

'Here is where I thought we might build our nest,' said the moorhen, showing his mate some thick rushes. She agreed at once. And then, what a happy time they had, the two of them! They were so pleased with one another, so glad to be together in the sunshine! The kingfishers too were very happy. They had made their home in the hole in the bank, and to it they often took the moorhens to show them how comfortable it was. But after a while the moorhens didn't like it. They said it smelt horrible.

So it did! For in the tunnel there were now a great many old fish bones and fishy pellets that the kingfishers had thrown up after digesting the fish they had eaten. These smelt nasty as they decayed, and the two moorhens could not bear the smell. But the kingfishers didn't mind. Fish was fish whether bad or good, and the smell seemed quite natural to them.

One day the kingfisher called excitedly to the moorhens, '*Kee kee kee!* Come and see! We have a nest and eggs now!'

So the moorhens went to see. They peered into the smelly tunnel, and saw the nest at the end – and it was made of old fish bones! *What a nest for young ones to hatch on!* thought the cleanly moorhens in disgust. There were five round eggs, and they gleamed white in the darkness of the tunnel. The mother kingfisher sat down proudly on her eggs again, settling herself comfortably on the fish bones.

'Come and see *our* nest now!' said the moorhens to the kingfisher. They swam off and the kingfisher followed. Certainly the moorhens' nest was a nice open-air affair after the smelly one in the tunnel. It was a platform made of flattened-out rushes, and it was right on the water itself. In the middle, the platform sank a little to hold the eggs. There were seven eggs there, buff-coloured with red spots, and they were large compared with the kingfishers'.

'It doesn't seem a very *safe* nest to me,' said the kingfisher doubtfully. 'Why, anyone could see it!'

'But nobody *has*!' said the moorhen as she clambered

up to the platform and sat on her eggs.

In the lovely summertime the moorhens' eggs hatched out into amusing little chicks. The kingfishers' eggs hatched too, but nobody saw the young ones for some time, for they were well hidden in the tunnel. Every one knew the moorhens' little black chicks, for before two weeks had passed they were swimming merrily about the pond, seven little black blobs with jerking heads! They followed their father and mother everywhere, and if either of their parents gave the alarm cry and scuttled over the water hurriedly to the reeds, the youngsters would see the white underparts of their parents' tails gleaming brightly and would follow quickly to a safe hiding place.

Each little bird had a hook-claw on one wing and when they needed to climb up to the platform nest they used this claw as a hand and could reach the nest easily. But one day when they climbed up, what a surprise! There were more eggs in the nest!

'You cannot sleep in the nest now,' said their father.

'I will build you another one nearby. Your mother needs the nest for her second family. You must help her now all you can.'

The little creatures settled happily down on the new nest, and were most excited when the second batch of eggs hatched out. '*Crek! Crek!*' cried one. 'I will go and find some food for our tiny brothers and sisters!'

Off went all the youngsters eagerly, and soon came back with titbits for the new family. By the next day there were seventeen moorhens – the two parents, seven of the first family, and eight new youngsters, who belonged to the second batch of eggs! How full the pond seemed! What a happy time all the little black moorchicks had, swimming about, calling to one another, bobbing here and there, diving to the bottom, finding food for themselves and the babies – and even helping to make another nest in case their mother laid a third batch of eggs! They were a very happy and contented family.

The chicks were taught many things, and the chief

lesson was how to swim underwater to escape an enemy. Their mother was very clever at this. She would bob down under the water and swim across the pond without showing herself at all. Then, at the other side, she would just put her red-marked bill above the water, and nothing else.

All the chicks practised this until they too could swim across the pond under water. The moorhens were so busy with their two families that they forgot all about the kingfishers – and then one morning, what a surprise! They saw five small kingfishers all sitting on an alder branch over the water, having their first lesson in fishing! The little kingfishers were proud and excited. They had often peeped out of their hole, but they had never fished for themselves before.

'*Kee, kee, kee!*' called their father, and he dived in to show them how to catch a fish. He flew up to the branch with a gleaming fish in his beak, but he would not give it to any of the hungry youngsters. He threw it back into the pond and it floated there, dead.

'Go and get it if you want it!' cried the kingfisher.

The five small kingfishers looked down hungrily. One of them suddenly opened his wings, dropped down to the water and snatched up the fish. Back to the branch he flew, excited and pleased. He ate the fish and looked down for another.

'Good!' said his father. 'Now try to catch a live fish, or even a fat tadpole. But remember this – knock your fish hard against a branch when you have caught it, for it is unpleasant to swallow a wriggling creature – and *always* swallow it head first, never tail first or it might stick in your throat!'

'But suppose we catch it tail first,' said a youngster. 'What shall we do?'

'I'll show you!' said the father and he dived in and caught another fish, this time tail first. He knocked it against a branch, threw it up into the air, neatly caught it *head* first and swallowed it! One by one the youngsters dived into the water and soon learnt how to catch fish for themselves. The moorhens enjoyed watching them. And then one day all the kingfishers called goodbye.

'*Kee kee kee!*' said the old kingfisher. 'There will not be enough food in this small pond for all you moorhens and so many kingfishers. So I am taking my family to the big river where there is more food than a hundred kingfishers can catch. Goodbye! *Kee kee kee!*'

'Goodbye! Goodbye!' cried all the moorhens at once. The kingfishers flew off, seven bright streaks of blue, and, although the moorhens saw them no more, they often heard them calling to one another from the river. '*Kee kee kee! Kee kee kee!*'

The Tail of Bup the Bunny

The Tail of Bup
the Bunny

THERE WAS once a bunny called Bup. He was very vain and longed for everyone to look at him and admire him. His whiskers were long, his ears were big and his fur was thick. The only thing he didn't like was his tail.

It was just a furry blob, like all rabbits' tails. But Bup wanted a big tail, one like Bushy the squirrel's, or a long one like Puss Cat's. It was horrid to have a little bobtail that nobody took any notice of at all.

Then, one day, when he was out in the woods, he found a lovely long white tail. It had belonged to a toy cat that a little boy had taken for a walk. The tail had caught in a bramble and fallen off, so the little boy had left it there.

Bup picked it up and looked at it. Here was exactly the kind of tail he had so often wanted. He would take it home, try it on, and see how it looked!

So off he went, *clippitty-clippitty* through the woods, and ran down his hole. When he was safely down there, he tied the long white tail on to his own, and then looked over his shoulder to see what it was like.

'My!' he said. 'I look grand! Yes, I do! I shall have this tail for my own, and pretend to everyone that it is real. No one will know, and they will all admire me and be jealous! I shall be the only rabbit with a long tail!'

He stayed in his hole for a few days, and when his friends came to see what was the matter, he put his head out and answered them very proudly.

'I am growing a long tail,' he said. 'I hear it's quite the fashion now. It's only half grown yet, but as soon as it is full-grown, I'll show it to you.'

Well, all the rabbits were most astonished. They asked each other whether anyone had heard of a long-tailed bunny before, but no one ever had. They began to think that Bup was making fun of them, so they waited anxiously for the day to come when he would come and play with them again.

On the seventh day Bup the bunny came out of his hole. He had tied on the toy cat's tail very firmly, so that it quite hid his own bobtail. As he lolloped out of his hole, all the rabbits cried out in surprise.

'Yes, he's grown a long tail! Yes, he has! Come and look, everybody! Bup has a long tail!'

Not only the rabbits came to see, but the foxes and weasels, sparrows and thrushes, hedgehogs and moles. The foxes and weasels were not allowed to come too near, for the rabbits hated them, but they came quite near enough to see the wonderful long tail.

How proud Bup was! He hopped about here and there, showing off his long tail, enjoying all the cries of surprise and envy.

'How did you do it, Bup?' asked the other rabbits. 'Tell us, and we will do the same.'

Bup knew quite well that they couldn't do the same because his was only a pretend tail. But he couldn't tell them that, of course, so he sat down and looked very wise.

'All you've got to do,' he said, 'is to sit at home in your burrow, think about tails for seven days, and then at the end of that time you will have one as good as mine.'

Well, the silly rabbits believed him! Off they all went to their burrows, and sat at home for seven days thinking of nothing but tails. But alas for them! When they came out again their tails were as short as ever! They were dreadfully disappointed.

'You are stupid creatures,' said Bup, curling his whiskers. 'I am the cleverest of all of you. Why don't you make me your king? It would be nice for you to have a long-tailed rabbit for a king, wouldn't it?'

Now, not many rabbits liked Bup, for he was so vain. But he was so determined to be king that at last they thought they had better make him their chief.

So they all set out to go to Breezy Hill where they held their important meetings. They sat round in a ring, with Bup in the middle and the oldest rabbit by him.

'Friends,' said the oldest rabbit. 'You are met together today to decide whether Bup the bunny shall be your king or not. He is the only long-tailed rabbit in our town. We have all tried to grow tails like his and we cannot. Therefore it seems as if he must be the cleverest among us. Shall we make him king?'

But before the listening rabbits could answer, a red fox came slinking up. He had smelt the rabbits from far off, and had come to see if he could pick one of them up for his dinner. They saw him coming over the hilltop, and with one frightened look they took to their heels and fled.

Bup fled too. His long tail dragged on the ground

behind him, but he had forgotten all about it. All he thought of was his hole, his lovely, safe, cosy hole! If only he could get there before the red fox caught him!

The fox chose to chase Bup, for he was fat and could not run quite so fast as the others. So off he went after poor Bup.

All the other rabbits reached their holes safely, and popped their heads out to watch the race. Nearer and nearer the fox came till he was almost on top of Bup. Then he suddenly made a snatch at the rabbit's long tail – and got it in his mouth!

'Oh! Oh! Now Bup is caught!' cried all the watching rabbits.

But the string that tied the long tail on to Bup suddenly broke, and Bup raced on free, while the astonished fox stopped still with the tail in his mouth.

'My! Oh my!' sang out the rabbits. 'Why, Bup's got a short tail as well as a long tail! Just look! There's his little bobtail, just like ours!'

So there was, quite plain to see, as Bup ran

helter-skelter for his hole. Down he popped in safety, and lay there panting. How glad he was that his long tail had only been a pretend one!

The fox gave one chew at the pretend tail and then blew it out of his mouth. Off he went in disgust. When he was safely out of sight, the rabbits all came crowding out to see the tail. They soon found out that it was nothing but a toy cat's tail, and how cross they were!

'To think that we all sat in our burrows for seven days, thinking of nothing but tails!' cried the oldest rabbit. 'And we nearly made that wicked rabbit our king!'

'And how foolish we should have been if we had grown long tails!' said another. 'Why, the fox would catch us easily if our tails were any longer!'

'Where's that stupid Bup Bunny?' cried all the rabbits. 'Let us go and find him!'

So off they went to Bup's burrow and dragged him out. They gave him a good scolding so that both his ears drooped, and his eyes filled with tears.

And that was the end of Bup being so vain. If ever he showed any signs of being proud again, someone would say to him, 'Well, Bup? Have you grown another long tail yet?'

And then Bup would go very red and run away!

The Funny Little Hedgehog

The Funny Little Hedgehog

ONE MORNING when Dick looked out of the window he saw something on the lawn that made him look and look again.

'Mother,' he said, 'there's something in the bottom of the net that goes all round the tennis court. What can it be?'

Mother looked. There certainly did seem to be something rolled up in the bottom of the brown net. 'Go and see what it is, Dick,' she said. So Dick ran out into the sunshine. He came to the net and bent down. At first he couldn't see at all what was rolled up in it – and then, when he put down his hand to feel, something pricked him!

'Gosh! It's a hedgehog!' said Dick in surprise. 'Poor thing. It's caught in the net. I'd better undo it.'

So Dick tried to undo the net from the hedgehog. The little, prickly creature was very frightened and curled himself up tightly. Dick could not get him untangled from the net at all.

'Mother!' he called. 'The prickles of the hedgehog are so tangled up in the net that I'll never be able to get him free. Shall I cut the net?'

'You'd better,' said his mother. 'But it is a pity, for it will quite spoil the net.'

Dick fetched some scissors and gently cut away the net from the frightened hedgehog. How tightly he had curled himself up! Dick couldn't see his head or his feet – only lots of brown prickles.

At last the hedgehog was free from the net. He lay on the grass, still curled up.

'Mother, he's very frightened!' said Dick. 'What can I do for him now? What will he eat?'

'Well, he usually eats beetles and grubs and things like that,' said Mother. 'But he will love a saucer of cat food, Dick. Go and get some from the kitchen.'

'Oh, Mother! Perhaps the hedgehog will get tame and live in our garden for always,' said Dick joyfully. 'I should like that. I shall call him Spiky!'

Dick put a saucer of cat food down by the hedgehog – but the little creature wouldn't uncurl himself at all. He just lay there like a brown prickly ball, not moving.

Dick moved away and hid behind a bush. Soon he saw the hedgehog move. A tiny brown nose looked out – two black eyes gazed around – then, when the hedgehog thought there was no one about, he uncurled the whole of himself and stood on his four short legs.

He sniffed. Ah! What was that nice smell? Cat food – what a treat! In a flash the hedgehog had got his head and front paws into the saucer, and was eating up the meaty food more quickly than a cat.

Dick was pleased. It was fun to see a little wild

animal behaving so tamely. The little boy made all sorts of plans. He would have him for a pet! He would teach him to come when he was called. What fun to see Spiky running up when his name was shouted!

But Spiky *wouldn't* be tamed. As soon as Dick got near him, he curled up tightly again. And when Dick left him to go to his dinner, Spiky hid himself so well that Dick couldn't find him at all afterwards. It was most disappointing.

But all the same the little hedgehog ate the tinned cat food that Dick put down each day. Dick couldn't think where Spiky had his home for he hardly ever saw him – and as the hedgehog came for his meal at night, he didn't see him feeding either.

Spiky lived in a cosy hole in the bank of the lane outside Dick's garden. There he had a fine home. In the winter he lined it with moss and dead leaves to keep it warm, and slept there soundly, his head in his paws. In the summer he used it for a hiding place and stayed there very often in the daytime, dozing.

He liked his hole. He had been very frightened when he had run into the tennis net and got caught. No matter how he had struggled he hadn't been able to get free – he had only got more tightly into the net.

Dick soon forgot to worry because Spiky wouldn't be a pet. He put down the tinned cat food each evening – and then something happened that put the hedgehog quite out of his head. A burglar came to the house one night and stole the rings belonging to Dick's mother! Just fancy that!

He only had time to take three rings, because Daddy heard him, shouted at him and frightened him. The robber jumped out of the window and ran away at top speed. Daddy ran after him and caught him. He called a policeman, and the robber was taken to prison – but will you believe it, when he got there he hadn't got those rings anywhere about him! His pockets were empty.

'He must have thrown them away as he ran,' said the policeman. 'We must hunt for them.' So everyone hunted all round about – in the garden, in the lane and down the road to the police station. But nobody found them. They just didn't seem to be anywhere at all. The burglar wouldn't say a word about them. He just said, untruthfully, that he hadn't taken any rings.

'He's put them somewhere,' said the policeman to Daddy. 'And he means to go and get them some time or other when you've forgotten all about them.'

'I do wonder where they are,' said Daddy and Mother and Dick a hundred times a day.

Do you know where they were? They were in a most extraordinary place. As the burglar had run down the lane he had stuffed the three rings into a hole in the bank – and it was the hedgehog's hole! Spiky wasn't there – it was night-time, and he liked to go hunting for beetles and grubs then. The burglar felt sure no one would find the rings there. He meant to get them afterwards. Daddy hadn't seen him do this because it was a dark night. But there the rings were, stuffed into Spiky's hole!

Now Spiky didn't go back to his hole for two or three days. He had found a splendid place for slugs in a garden some way away, and was enjoying himself very much. He fed on fat slugs all night long and then, instead of going back to his hole, he curled himself up in a flowerpot and slept during the daytime.

When at last he did go back to his hole in the bank, one early summer morning, he was surprised to find something there that hadn't been there before. Three shining rings! They could not be eaten – they were too hard. Spiky didn't like them. He was afraid of strange things. He sniffed and sniffed and sniffed at the rings, and then crawled into his hole, trying to get behind them so that he need not touch them.

But the hole was small and Spiky had to lie on top of them. He didn't like it. He grew angry in his little hedgehog mind. He could not go to sleep because he was worried about the strange shining things in his hole.

I'll push them out! thought Spiky suddenly. *Of course!*

I'll push them out! I won't have them in. This is my *hole!*
I won't have strange things walking in.

Just as he was about to push out the rings, he heard
a noise of footsteps coming down the lane. He listened
and heard Dick's voice, talking to his mother. Ah!
He was not afraid of Dick. Spiky took a ring in his
mouth and pushed aside the curtain of moss that
hung over the entrance to the hole. He dropped the
ring out. Then he went back for the next one, and
dropped that out too.

And at that very moment Dick came walking
down the lane with his mother. His sharp eyes caught
sight of something gleaming on the bank and he gave
a shout.

'Mother! Look! Is that one of your rings? Oh!
There are two!'

Even as Dick bent down to pick up the rings, he
saw the hedgehog's snout poking out of the hole, and
in Spiky's mouth was the third ring. The hedgehog
dropped it and it rolled down the bank. Then the

curtain of moss fell over the entrance of the hole and Spiky disappeared.

'Mother! Oh, Mother! Spiky had the rings in his hole!' shouted Dick. 'And he waited until I passed by – and then he dropped them out for me. Oh, Mother, isn't he a wonderful hedgehog! I'm glad I was kind to him. I'm glad I rescued him from the tennis net and gave him food each night. He's paid me back for it, hasn't he?'

'Well, it certainly looks like it,' said Mother, most astonished. She took her rings in delight. They were not a bit spoilt.

'To think they were in Spiky's hole all the time!' said Dick. 'I expect the hedgehog found them and took them there to keep safely until he could give them to me, Mother.'

'No, I don't think that,' said Mother. 'I expect the thief stuffed them into the hole, not knowing it belonged to a hedgehog who would throw them out.'

'Good old Spiky!' shouted Dick, dancing around in

delight. 'I was a friend to you and now you're a friend to me. I wish I could take your photograph and send it to the newspapers. You ought to be famous.'

But Spiky didn't like the sound of that. He disappeared from his hole when next Dick went to look for him, and now he is wandering about in someone else's garden. He may be in yours! Be kind to him, won't you!

Susan and the Birds

Susan and the Birds

SUSAN WAS very fond of the birds in the garden. She badly wanted to get near to them and watch them. But whenever she crept close, they flew away.

'It's such a pity, Mummy,' she said. 'I only want to watch them, and see how pretty they are, and find out what bird sings so sweetly – but they won't let me. It isn't kind of them to keep flying away. Don't they know I'm their friend?'

'Well, no, they don't, darling,' said her mother. 'You see, most people don't bother about watching the birds, they just frighten them away – so they think you are the same.'

'But I'm not,' said Susan. 'I want to be friends with them – but they won't be friends with me!'

'Well, you must make them tame,' said her mother. 'Then they will let you come near them.'

'How can I make them tame?' said Susan. 'Tell me, and I will.'

'We will give them a bird table,' said her mother. 'They will love that. It is wintertime now, and all the birds that eat insects are hungry, because there are so few flies and grubs to be found. They will soon come to your table, and then you can watch them closely.'

So Mother made Susan a bird table. It was very easy to make. First Mother took a square piece of board. That was for the top of the table. Then she found an old broom handle, rather long. That was for the leg. She nailed the square bit of board to the broom handle, and then drove the other end of the handle into the ground.

'There's your table for the birds!' she said to Susan. 'Now, if you spread it with bits of food each day, you will soon make friends with the birds!'

The table was very near Susan's playroom window. She was pleased. 'I can sit in the window and watch the birds hop on to the table easily,' she said. 'Mummy, what shall I put on it? Anything else besides food?'

'Well, the birds would like a few twigs nailed behind the table, I think,' said Mother. 'Then they can perch on those when they fly down. And you should put a bowl of water out too, Susan. They have to drink as well as to eat – and on a nice fine day they may bathe in the water too.'

Susan couldn't help feeling excited. She put a bowl of water on the table, and then she found a few nice twigs in the hedge. With her little hammer and a few nails, she nailed the twigs to the back of the table. Now it was ready!

'What do the birds like to eat?' she asked. 'I know some of them like insects, but I can't give them those. Most of them like soaked bread, don't they, Mummy?'

'Yes. You can give them that – and any crumbs

from the tablecloth and bread bin – and the scrapings from the milk-pudding dish,' said Mother.

So Susan put those out on the bird table. Then she went into her playroom, hid behind the curtain and watched.

The sparrows saw the food there first. They talked about it quite a lot in the trees nearby, and wondered if they dared to go down and try it.

'There is no cat about,' said a brown sparrow. 'Let's go. I'll fly down first and then chirrup to you if it is safe.'

So he flew down to the twigs at the back of the bird table, and had a look at the food. It looked very good to him! He flew down on to the table and pecked at the bread.

'The first bird on my table!' said Susan in joy. 'What a little dear he is, with his brown coat and dark head!'

'Chirrup, chirrup!' said the sparrow, and at once two or three more flew down to peck at the soaked bread. Soon the table was quite full of the noisy little birds.

Susan pressed her nose close to the windowpane. The birds saw her, and flew away in fright. But another little bird flew down at once and gave a little trill.

'Oh – a robin!' said Susan. 'A lovely redbreast. Look at his red breast, Mummy, and his bright black eyes, and long, thin legs. Isn't he lovely? And, oh, what a rich little song he has!'

The robin pecked at the bits of milk pudding and the bread. When two or three sparrows flew down again he flew off. 'He doesn't like to mix with the noisy sparrows,' said Mother, who had come to watch too. 'Ah, look – here's a lovely big bird, Susan. What is it?'

'A blackbird, of course!' said Susan. 'Everyone knows him!'

He was a black glossy fellow, much bigger than the sparrows. He drove them away and began to peck up the bread and the pudding greedily. While he was eating it a bird as big as he was flew down and joined him.

It was brown and had speckles all over its chest.

'What is it?' asked Susan.

'A thrush, of course!' said Mother. 'Look at the freckles on his breast. You can always tell a thrush by those – and both he and the blackbird have lovely songs too. You will hear them in the springtime.'

'That's four different kinds of birds already,' said Susan. 'Oh, Mummy, my bird table *is* going to be fun!'

'We'll put something else on the table tomorrow,' said Mother. 'Then one or two other birds will come.'

So the next day Mother gave Susan two bones, one to hang from the table and the other to put *on* the table.

'Why should I hang one on string?' asked Susan.

'For the tits,' said Mother. 'They like to swing on their food – so they can swing on this bone. But the big starlings like to stand on their bone – so you can just lay that one on the table for them.'

It was great fun to watch for the little tits and the

merry starlings. The tits came first. They were pretty little birds, with blue caps on their heads, and blue and yellow coats.

'Blue tits,' said Mother. 'You may perhaps see the great tit too. He wears a black cap, and is bigger, so you will know him when he comes. See how those blue tits stand upside down on their bone and swing to and fro. Aren't they enjoying it!'

It was great fun to watch the tits, but it was even more fun to watch the starlings. They were bigger than the tits and sparrows, but not so big as the blackbird. They were greedy, noisy, bad-mannered birds, dressed in feathers that shone blue and green and purple.

'Oh, look how they peck one another, and call each other rude names!' said Susan. 'Oh, Mummy, that one has pushed the other off the table! No, he's back again – and he's pushed the first one off the bone, and now a third one is trying his hardest to drag the bone away!'

The starlings chattered and squawked, pecked and quarrelled. It was really funny to watch them. Some sparrows came down to join in the fun, and the blackbird turned up, but flew away because the table was too crowded.

'I do like my bird table!' said Susan. 'It's the greatest fun, Mummy. The birds don't seem to mind me peeping at them now either. They must know that it is I who put the food out for them!'

The birds sipped the water, and once the robin had a bath in it. He splashed the water all over himself. It was sweet to watch him.

'Now we will put out something for a few seed-eating birds,' said Mummy. 'I would like you to see the pretty chaffinch, Susan. He will come if we get a few seeds for him.'

So they bought a mixture of birdseed and put some on the table. The sparrows found the seeds at once and pecked them up greedily.

'Their beaks are very good for breaking up the

seeds,' said Susan, watching them. 'They have big, strong beaks, haven't they, Mummy?'

'So has the chaffinch, if only he would come and show us his beak!' said Mummy. 'Ah – good – there he is! Now see how pretty he is, Susan, with his bright pink breast and the white bars on his wings, that flash when he flies!'

'*Pink pink!*' said the chaffinch, as he flew down to the table for the first time. 'Seeds for me! *Pink pink!*'

He took some in his strong beak and cracked them well. Susan saw that he had just the same kind of beak as the sparrows, but he was a neater, prettier bird. His little wife flew down to the table too, but she hadn't his beautiful pink breast.

'Mummy, I know heaps of birds now,' said Susan. 'And I shall get to know lots more, shan't I? Mummy, do you think the birds are pleased with their bird table?'

'Very pleased,' said Mother. 'And they will pay you back for your kindness in the spring, Susan!'

They did! The thrush sang his song over and over again to her. The blackbird fluted in his wonderful voice. The robin sang in little trills. The chaffinch carolled loudly. It was wonderful to hear them all!

'Thank you!' said Susan. 'You have paid me well for your table!'

Do have a table for the birds too. You will love it just as much as Susan did.

The Ugly Old
Toad

The Ugly Old Toad

ONCE UPON a time a big, old toad wanted to cross the road to get to a pond he knew on the other side. He couldn't jump high and quickly like his cousin the frog. He could only do small hops, or crawl, but he set off valiantly, hoping to get across the road before anything came along.

He was almost across when a horse and cart came down the lane. *Clippitty-cloppitty, clippitty-cloppitty* went the horse's hoofs, and the old toad heard them. He tried to hop away quickly, but one of the horse's hoofs trod on his back leg. Almost at once the horse lifted up his hoof again and went on, not knowing that he had crushed the foot of the toad.

'Oh!' groaned the toad to himself, crawling to the side of the road, dragging his hurt foot behind him. 'What a bit of bad luck! I can hardly walk now. How my foot is hurting me!' He was in such pain that he could not go any further. He squatted by the side of the road, hoping that his foot would soon get better. But it didn't.

He tried again to crawl, but his foot hurt him too much, so he lay there, half hidden by a tuft of grass, hoping that no enemy would come by.

The big rat ran by and stopped when he saw the toad. *Aha! Dinner for me!* thought the rat, knowing that the toad was hurt. He ran up to the toad and snapped at him.

The toad still could not crawl away, but he had a good trick to play on the rat. He oozed out an evil-smelling, horrible-tasting liquid all over his back. When the rat tried to bite him, he got his mouth full of the nasty stuff.

'Horrible!' said the rat, and stood staring at the toad with his mouth open, trying to let the nasty-tasting stuff drip out of his mouth. 'Horrible! I wouldn't have you for my dinner for anything!'

He ran off, and the toad sat still, glad to be rid of him. Then he heard footsteps coming down the lane, and he shrank back into the grass, trying to look like a brown clod of earth. He really did look like one.

Soon a boy came up, whistling. He almost trod on the toad, but he did not see him and went whistling on. He thought the old toad was just a lump of earth.

He stayed still, hoping that his foot would stop hurting. But the horse's hoof had been hard and heavy – it was a wonder it had not cut the toad's foot right off.

Then the toad heard more footsteps – lighter ones this time. He crouched down again, but this time the passerby was sharper-eyed than the boy.

'Ooh! A toad!' said a voice, and the toad, looking up cautiously, saw a little girl gazing down at him.

She wrinkled her nose in disgust.

'Nasty creature! I can't bear toads! Ugly thing with your pimply back and your creepy-crawly ways! I don't like you a bit!'

The toad crouched very still. He was afraid. This little girl might stamp on him – children were sometimes very cruel to creatures like him. But he couldn't help being an ugly old toad – he was born like that.

However, the little girl did not stamp on him. She wasn't cruel. She did think the toad was ugly, and she didn't like him much, but she wasn't going to be unkind.

'I don't like ugly creatures,' she said to the toad. 'I couldn't bear to touch you. Oooh, that would be horrid! It would make me feel ill.'

The toad was sad. He wished he had been born a butterfly or a bird. Then perhaps the little girl would have liked him. But you had to be what you were born to be – there wasn't any help for it. Then suddenly the little girl saw the toad's foot. It was all crushed and flattened. She stared at it in horror.

'Toad! Your foot is squashed to bits! Is it hurting you? Oh, how did that happen? Did someone tread on you?'

The toad still crouched flat. He knew the little girl wouldn't tread on him now, but he was still afraid. She looked at him, sad because of his foot.

'Oh, I can't leave you here like this,' she said. 'I'm sorry I said all those unkind things now. I didn't know you were hurt. I think I had better take you home to my mother – she will know what to do with your foot.'

The toad didn't want to be taken home. He wanted to be left alone in peace. The little girl was wondering how to carry him.

'Although I am very sorry for you, I simply can't touch you,' she said. 'I can't! I should drop you if I touched you. You see, I don't like toads.'

Then she thought of using her handkerchief. She would wrap the toad in that and carry him by taking hold of the four corners of the hanky. Then she would not need to touch him at all.

So to the toad's surprise and fright, she dropped her hanky over him, rolled him gently into it, and picked him up in the hanky. She carried him by taking hold of the four corners, but she didn't even like doing that!

She took him home. The toad did not wriggle or struggle, because it hurt his foot too much. He just lay in the hanky, very miserable, wondering what was going to happen to him.

The little girl went in at her gate. She called to her mother. 'Mummy! I've got a hurt toad. Can you do something for him?'

Her mother was very surprised. She undid the hanky and took the toad in her bare hands. She didn't mind touching any creature. She saw the hurt foot and was sorry.

'I can't do much,' she said. 'I will just bathe his foot with very weak iodine – but it's no good binding it up.

The best thing you can do for him, Jenny, is to put him in a cool, shady corner of the garden, somewhere where there are plenty of flies for him to catch, and leave him to himself. Maybe the foot will heal itself.'

'I don't like him much,' said Jenny.

'He can't help being a toad,' said her mother. 'You might have been born a toad – and think how sad you would be if people hated you, and tried to hurt you because you happened to be ugly. That's not fair, Jenny.'

'No, it isn't,' said Jenny. She looked down at the toad, and he looked up at her. She saw his eyes.

'Mummy, he's got the most beautiful eyes!' she said, surprised. 'Do look at them. They are like jewels in his head, gleaming as bright as copper.'

'All toads have lovely eyes,' said Mother. 'They are nice creatures, Jenny, and make good pets.'

'Oh, no, Mummy!' said Jenny, astonished. 'I have never heard of a toad as a pet before!'

'There are quite a lot of things you haven't heard

of!' said Jenny's mother. 'Now, I've finished bathing his foot – do you think you can possibly bring yourself to carry him in your hands to a nice bit of the garden – or do you dislike toads so much?'

Jenny felt a bit ashamed of herself. She looked down at the toad. His coppery eyes gleamed kindly at her. He looked patient and wise.

'I'll carry him,' she said, and she picked him up gently in her hands. He kept quite still. Jenny took him down the garden and put him in the cool hedge behind her father's lettuces.

'There you are!' she said. 'Stay there and catch flies. I don't know what else you eat, but there are heaps of flies here for you.'

There were. The toad heard a big one buzzing just over his head. He looked at it – and then, quick as a flash, he shot out a long, sticky tongue, caught the fly on the tip of it, swallowed, and looked at Jenny.

'A good meal,' he seemed to say.

146

Jenny laughed. 'You're rather nice,' she said, and left him.

She forgot all about him. A week went by, then two weeks. Then Daddy came in one evening, bringing two delicious lettuces for supper.

'Good gracious!' said Jenny's mother, pleased. 'I thought you told me that all your lettuces had been eaten by slugs. What beauties these are!'

'Ah! I've got someone to guard my lettuces for me!' said Father. 'And a very good fellow he is too. He never allows a single slug on my lettuce bed now.'

'Who is he?' said Jenny, puzzled.

'He's a toad,' said her father, 'a wise, friendly, kind old toad. He lives in the hedge behind my kitchen garden, and he keeps guard over the lettuces. See how well they have grown since the old toad looked after them for me!'

'Daddy! He must be my toad! I forgot all about him,' said Jenny, excited.

'Your toad? I thought you didn't like toads,' said

her father. 'What do you mean?'

Jenny told him. 'And we shall know if it is my toad by his foot,' she said. 'Has he got a mended foot, Daddy?'

'I didn't notice,' said Father. 'Let's go and see.'

So they went to see – and there was the old toad, and behind him was his hurt foot – mended and healed now, but rather a funny shape.

'It is my toad!' said Jenny. 'Look, he's crawling over to me, Daddy. He knows I'm the little girl who brought him home.'

'Tickle his back with a grass,' said Father. 'He'll like that.'

So Jenny did, and the toad liked it very much. He tried to scratch his back with one of his feet, and made Jenny laugh.

'You're a good old toad,' she said. 'I like you, and you shall be my pet.'

He is her pet, and he still keeps guard over the kitchen garden. I know because I've seen him there!

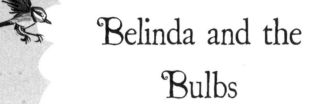

Belinda and the Bulbs

Belinda and the Bulbs

'WHAT ARE we going to buy when we go out this morning, Nurse?' asked Belinda.

'We've got to go to the flower nursery and get some bulbs for your mummy to plant in her bowls,' said Nurse. 'We shall get lots of daffodils, because Mummy is so fond of those.'

'I wish she'd let me plant them for her,' said Belinda. 'I'd love to play about with that earthy stuff they plant them in, and pack it all into the bowls.'

'Well, if you're a good girl, I'll ask Mummy if she'll let you help,' said Nurse.

But wasn't it a pity, Belinda wasn't a good girl at

all! She stepped right into the middle of three puddles, she rubbed her nice clean gloves in some wet paint, and she ran across the road without holding Nurse's hand.

'Well, you're just about as naughty as you can be this morning!' said Nurse crossly. 'I don't know what's the matter with you – really I don't! I certainly shan't ask your mummy to let you help with the bulbs, Belinda.'

'Well, I shall help with them, all the same!' said Belinda rudely.

Nurse bought a big bag of daffodil bulbs and then went to the grocer's. She bought some bacon, some onions and some soap. Then she turned homewards, her basket quite full.

Belinda sulked all the way home, so Nurse said nothing to her, thinking she really was a naughty little girl this morning. When they reached home Nurse put her basket down in the hall and then sent Belinda upstairs to tidy her hair.

'You'd better sit down quietly with your sewing,' said Nurse. 'I'm going in to ask Mummy about your new frocks.'

'I want to come too, and ask her if I can help to plant the bulbs,' said Belinda.

'Well, you can't,' said Nurse. 'You've been much too naughty. Go straight upstairs and do as you're told.'

Belinda ran upstairs crossly. As soon as she heard Nurse go into the drawing room to talk to Mummy, she crept down again and went to the basket that Nurse had left in the hall.

'I will plant those bulbs!' she said to herself. 'I'll take them now, and get some earth from the garden. Then I'll find Mummy's four big bowls and plant them all. Nurse can't stop me if I've already done them!'

She opened a paper bag that she found in Nurse's shopping basket, and peeped inside.

'These are the bulbs!' she said. 'Good! I'll put

them in the nursery, and then I'll go outside and get some earth!'

She hid the bag in the nursery, then ran downstairs and out into the garden. She filled a wooden garden basket with earth and carried it upstairs. She had to fill it twice before she had enough for the four big bowls. Then she emptied the bulbs out of the bag.

'Now I'll plant them!' said Belinda. 'Oh dear, I do hope I'll have time before Nurse comes back.'

She pushed the little brown things into the earth, and soon each bowl held about six bulbs.

'Now I'll put them in a dark cupboard, just like Mummy did last year,' said Belinda. 'Nurse will never know I've planted them – not till Mummy asks, and then won't Nurse be cross to think I've planted them after all!'

She carried them to the dark cupboard on the landing and put them on the shelf inside. Then she shut the door, ran back to the nursery, and took out her sewing. When Nurse came back, she was sitting quietly on her chair.

Mummy came with Nurse, and she kissed Belinda. 'I hope you've been a good girl this morning,' she said. Belinda said nothing, but went very red.

'Did you bring me some daffodil bulbs to plant in my bowls, Nurse?' said Mummy.

'Yes, I did,' said Nurse. 'They're here in my basket.'

To Belinda's great surprise, Nurse took a bag from her basket and gave it to Mummy. Mummy opened it and looked inside.

'Oh, they're beautiful daffy bulbs,' she said. 'I think I'll plant them now, while I remember it. I'll go and get my bowls.'

Belinda stared at Mummy in surprise, as she emptied a large pile of bulbs on to the nursery table. What a funny thing. Why, she had only just planted the bulbs herself, and now here were some more!

Mummy went to the shelf where she kept her bowls, and found they were not there.

'Why, that's funny!' she said. 'Where are my bowls?'

Belinda began to feel very uncomfortable. She wished she hadn't been so naughty. What was she to say to Mummy? Then Nurse gave a cry of astonishment.

'Why!' she said, 'where are the onions I bought this morning? I know I put them in the basket, and they're not here now. Cook specially wants them for dinner – I do hope I haven't lost them.'

'Well, I seem to have lost my bowls, and you've lost your onions,' said Mummy with a laugh. 'We are unlucky.'

Just then Cook put her head in at the door.

'Please, Madam,' she said, 'I want to put some jars of jam on that shelf in the landing cupboard, and I see there are some bowls there. May I move them?'

'Bowls!' said Mummy in surprise. 'However did they get there?'

She went to see, and came back carrying two. Cook came behind, carrying two more. Mummy put them down on the table, looking very puzzled.

Belinda wanted to speak, but somehow her tongue wouldn't say anything.

Mummy turned to Nurse. 'Here are my bowls!' she said. 'And it looks as if something is planted in them. Do you know anything about it?'

'No, I don't,' said Nurse, surprised. 'What's in the bowls, do you think?'

Mummy dug her hand into the earth – and pulled out an onion!

'Good gracious me!' she cried. 'Here's an onion! And here's another – and another – and another! Why, bless us all, the bowls are planted with onions!'

'They're the onions I bought this morning!' said Nurse, and she took them one by one from the bowls.

'How did they get there?' said Mummy in rather a stern voice. 'Belinda, do you know anything about this?'

'Yes,' said Belinda in a very small voice. 'I thought they were daffodil bulbs and I planted them in your bowls.'

'Well, they're onion bulbs,' said Mummy. 'Why didn't you wait to ask me if you could help, before you did this silly thing?'

Belinda didn't answer, so Nurse explained to Mummy.

'Belinda wasn't a good girl this morning,' she said, 'and I said that I should tell you she mustn't help you to plant the bulbs. I suppose she thought she would do it all the same.'

'So you went to take the bulbs out of Nurse's basket, and took the onions instead!' said Mummy. 'Well, that was a clever thing to do! Whoever heard of anyone planting onions in bowls before!'

Belinda burst into tears. She did feel such a silly girl, especially when she saw that Mummy and Nurse were laughing at her.

'I'm sorry, Mummy!' she said. 'I thought they were daffodils. Don't laugh at me any more.'

'You deserve to be laughed at,' said Mummy. 'Come here and empty out this earth and take it back to the garden. Bulbs have to be planted in special fibre, not earth. You have given yourself a lot of trouble for nothing!'

Belinda did as she was told. She felt very upset, and soon she whispered to Nurse that she was sorry she had been naughty. Then she whispered it to Mummy.

'Oh, well, you've had your punishment,' said Mummy, smiling. 'Look, here's one more bowl left. You shall plant real daffodil bulbs in it this time!'

So Belinda did, and felt happy again.

'Isn't it a good thing Cook didn't cook the daffodil bulbs for dinner!' she said.

'It certainly is,' said Mummy. 'But I think Cook knows the difference between daffy bulbs and onions, even if you don't, Belinda!'

Sly the Squirrel Gets a Shock

Sly the Squirrel Gets a Shock

SLY THE squirrel was a mean creature. He always got the very best nuts for himself. He wouldn't let the nuthatch have a single one of the nuts in the hazel wood where he lived, and if he caught the little dormouse taking one off the ground, he would bound down and chatter at him angrily.

'They're my nuts, they're my nuts!'

'They're not,' said the dormouse. 'You ask the hazel trees. They grow them for anyone.'

'The squirrel is a meanie, the squirrel is a meanie,' said the nuthatch, and whistled loud and long.

'Sly is his name and Sly is his nature!' sang a little

blue tit who sometimes liked a nut himself.

'Nobody likes the squirrel, nobody likes the squirrel!' squeaked the field mouse, popping his head up from a hole under the roots of a pine tree not far off. The squirrel stared round angrily. It wasn't nice to have things like that shouted out about him. He was very annoyed.

He bounded away to the top of a tree. It was late autumn, and there were many nuts hanging on the boughs. The squirrel picked one and bit it with his sharp teeth. He gnawed a hole in the nut to get at the sweet kernel.

But the kernel inside was not sweet. It was very bitter. The squirrel spat it out in disgust.

'A bad nut!' he said. 'There are such a lot this year. I wish the nuthatch and the mice would get all the bad nuts, and I could have all the good ones. That would serve them right for being so mean to me.'

As he sat and nibbled at a good nut, an idea came into his sly head.

'I know what I'll do! I'll gather all the bad nuts I can find and put them into a pile, and I'll tell the nuthatch and the mice I've picked a present for them! Then they will be sorry they called me rude names and will think I am a fine fellow. But what a shock they will get in the middle of the winter when they go to their store of nuts and find that they are all bad!'

The mean little squirrel began to hunt for the bad nuts. He knew that they had little holes in them where the nut-grub had bitten its way out. He put them all together in a pile at the foot of one of the hazel trees.

'Look at Sly the squirrel! He is piling up heaps of nuts for himself!' said the nuthatch to the dormouse below.

The squirrel overheard him. 'Those lovely nuts are not for myself,' he said. 'They are for you, and the dormouse and the field mouse.'

'I don't want them,' said the dormouse. 'I sleep all the winter through. I'm eating nuts myself now to get my body fat, so that I shall be able to sleep in comfort all the winter. It will soon be very cold weather.'

The nuthatch was surprised to hear that Sly the squirrel had collected the nuts for the others, and not for himself.

'Thank you,' he said. 'I may visit the pile in the winter.'

'I've plenty stored up for myself,' said the field mouse. 'But maybe I'll find a few of your nuts useful, Sly. Thank you very much. The nuthatch and I will cover them with leaves.'

So he and the nuthatch covered up the big pile of bad nuts with leaves.

Sly the squirrel grinned to himself. 'What a shock they will get!' he said.

Now that night the frost came. It came very suddenly indeed, before Sly the squirrel expected it. He had been so busy collecting nuts for the others that he had had no time to collect good ones for himself. Usually he picked many nuts and hid them in corners and crannies, so that when he awoke on a warm day in the winter and felt hungry, he would have plenty of nuts to find and eat.

It was terribly cold the next day. Sly woke up and looked out from his hole in the tree. 'I'd better go out and find some nuts to store away,' he said sleepily. He put his nose out a bit further, but the frost bit it and he drew it in again quickly.

'Oh! How cold! I'll sleep a bit longer!'

He slept for more than a month! When he did wake, he was dreadfully hungry. He leapt out of his hole into the winter sunshine. It was quite a warm day for wintertime.

He looked about for nuts. The trees were quite bare. There were no leaves and no nuts. And then Sly remembered that he had not had time to store away any good nuts at all!

'Oh my! I didn't put away nuts for myself as I usually do!' he said to himself. 'Now what shall I do?'

He sat hugging his little, empty tummy and then he

saw the nuthatch flying by, whistling.

'Hi, nuthatch! Where are there any nuts?'

'Nowhere,' said the bird. 'The trees are bare.'

Then Sly saw the little mouse. 'Hi, field mouse!' he called. 'Have you any nuts stored up? Could you spare me a few?'

'No, I've only enough for myself and my family,' said the field mouse. 'But have you forgotten that lovely pile over there – under those dead leaves?'

Sly had forgotten all about them. 'Where are they?' he said eagerly.

'You can have them all,' said the mouse. 'They are just over there.'

So Sly bounded over to the pile and brushed aside the leaves. He cracked the nuts hungrily.

But alas for the poor squirrel! Every nut was bad, every single one! The little field mouse ran up and the nuthatch flew down.

'What's the matter?' they said, as they saw Sly throwing away one nut after another without eating it.

'Bad, bad, all bad!' said Sly. 'Why did you collect all bad nuts, you silly stupid things?'

The nuthatch whistled and the field mouse squealed with laughter.

'Silly yourself! It was you who collected that pile of nuts and gave them to us. Don't you remember?'

And then at last Sly did remember! Yes, he had picked all those bad nuts – with holes in – to give the nuthatch and the field mouse a really horrid shock.

The nuthatch and the field mouse went off laughing. 'Serves you right!' they cried.

So Sly the squirrel had to go hungry all that winter, and if the little field mouse hadn't been kind and given him a few of his own nuts, he would have starved. I don't think he'll play a trick like that again, do you?

Lightwing the
Swallow

Lightwing the Swallow

LIGHTWING CAME out of a white egg in a nest made of mud. He was very tiny indeed, and at first he could see nothing in the dark barn where his mother and father had built their nest. But very soon his eyes made out the high rafters above him, and the beam on which his nest was put.

He looked at a hole in the barn roof through which he could see the blue sky. It was summertime, so the sky was often blue. Lightwing crouched down in the nest with his brother and sister, and waited impatiently for his mother and father to come with titbits to eat.

He was a funny little thing, rather bare, with very

few feathers at first. But gradually they grew, and soon Lightwing and his brother and sister were fluffy nestlings, sitting with ever-open beaks waiting for flies that their parents caught on the wing outside the big barn.

Lightwing was a swallow. He had a marvellous steel-blue back, a white vest and a streak of chestnut-red across his chest. His legs were small and his beak was wide in its gape. His wings were long and his tail was forked prettily. He longed for the day to come when he might fly off with his father and mother.

But when the day came he was rather afraid! His brother flew out of the nest and through the door as if he had been used to flying all his short life – but Lightwing and his sister sat on the edge of the nest, trembling. Their mother suddenly flew behind them and tipped them off the nest!

Lightwing fell – but as he fell he opened his wings, and lo and behold he could fly! His wings flashed through the barn door – he was up in the air and away, rejoicing to be in the clear, sunny blue sky.

He learnt to catch flies on the wing with his mouth wide open. He learnt to skim the water and pick up the flies hovering over the surface. He knew that when rain was coming the flies flew lower, and he followed them. When the weather was fine the flies flew high, and Lightwing soared below the clouds, following his food there. Then people said, 'The swallows fly high – it will be fine,' or, 'The swallows fly low – there will be rain.'

Lightwing grew strong and tireless as he flew throughout the warm summer days. But one night there was a chill in the air. Lightwing was surprised. He did not like it.

'Winter is coming!' sang the robin in his creamy voice.

'What is winter?' cried Lightwing in his pretty twitter. 'Is it something to eat?'

One night a chill north-west wind began to blow.

Lightwing felt restless. He wanted to fly somewhere, but he did not know where. He wanted to go where he could no longer feel the cold wind. He flew to the barn roof to ask his friends what to do. Hundreds of swallows settled on the old red roof. They chattered and twittered restlessly. The wind blew behind them.

And then, quite suddenly, a few swallows rose up into the air and flew southwards, with the chill wind behind them. In a few moments all the waiting hundreds had risen too, and with one accord flew to the south.

'Goodbye!' called the robin. 'Goodbye till the spring!'

Lightwing called goodbye and flew with the others. Over land and over sea sped the swallows, as fast as express trains, to a warmer southern land, where flies were plentiful and the sun was hot.

And there Lightwing is now – but when the spring comes again he will return, and maybe build his nest in your barn or mine!

The Elm Tree and
the Willow

The Elm Tree and the Willow

SIDE BY side in the hedge grew a great elm and a sapling willow. The willow was growing in the shade of the elm, and it did not get enough light or sunshine, but it did the best it could. It sent its thin roots down into the earth to look for water, and it put out long shoots to try to reach the sunshine.

The big elm scorned the small willow. It raised its head very high in the air, it grew thousands of small leaves, and in the wind it made such a rushing noise that it drowned the voice of the little willow.

The willow sometimes spoke timidly to the tall elm. It asked the great tree questions about the birds that nested every year in the bushy trunk of the elm. It admired the pretty red blossoms that grew on the big tree's twigs in the early spring, and which it flung down to the ground when the wind blew.

'Ah, you should grow blossoms like mine!' said the elm. 'Look at your silly little green catkins! And, see, when the autumn comes I send thousands of winged fruits spinning through the air for the children to catch. They love me – I am tall and grand, my leaves shout in the wind, I give welcome shade in the hot summer – but you are a miserable little thing!'

'Well, I cannot grow very big because you take so much light and sunshine from me,' said the willow humbly. 'But, great elm tree, I believe my roots go further down than yours do.'

'Pooh! What do roots matter!' said the elm tree impatiently. 'They don't show, do they?'

Now that autumn there came a great gale one dark, stormy night. The wind rushed through the trees, and the elm shouted so loudly that the willow was nearly deafened. The great tree swayed to and fro, and the willow bent too. The wind grew wilder and wilder, and the elm shouted more and more loudly – and then suddenly a terrifying thing happened.

The great elm bent so far over that it could not get its trunk back straight again. Its poor, weak roots could not hold it, and they broke. The tree gave a loud moaning cry and toppled heavily to the ground.

The willow was left alone to bear the strong gusts of wind. It was frightened. If the elm had fallen, surely it too would fall, for it was but a small tree. The wind pulled hard at it, but the willow's roots were deep and held it well. When the storm at last died down, the willow was still standing – and by it lay the great elm, its leaves dying by the thousand.

The wind came by once more and whispered to the willow, 'Roots don't show, but they matter most of all! Roots don't show, but they matter most of all!'

Black Bibs

Black Bibs

ONCE UPON a time, at the beginning of the New Year, the little brown house sparrows noticed that the starlings were growing beautiful green, violet and purple colours in their feathers. They saw that the little chaffinch had put on a much brighter pink waistcoat, and that the blackbird seemed to have dipped his beak in gold.

'Why?' they said to the starlings. 'Why?' to the chaffinch, and 'Why?' to the blackbird.

'Because spring is coming!' they all answered. 'We shall soon be looking for wives – and we like to be dressed in our best then! Why don't *you* do something about it, sparrows? Cock and hen sparrows are exactly the same in the way they dress! You might at least try to dress a little differently in springtime, so that when you go wooing your mates they may think you look handsome!'

'That is a good idea,' said the cock sparrows. 'We will go to Dabble the elf and ask her if she'll use her dyes to colour our feathers a bit!'

So they flew off to Dabble. She was indoors and the house was shut. The sparrows hopped up the path, and were just going to ring the bell when one said, 'We haven't yet decided what colour to ask for.'

'We'll have red vests,' said a big cock sparrow.

'Silly idea!' said another. 'We don't want to look like those stuck-up robins.'

'Well, let's have yellow tails and green beaks,' said another.

'And be laughed at by everyone!' screamed a fourth sparrow. 'No, we'll have blue wings and blue chests – very smart indeed.'

'I want pink legs, I want pink legs,' chirruped another.

'Be quiet and don't be silly,' said the one next to him. 'Do you want to look as if you're walking on primrose stalks? They're pink too.'

'Chirrup, chirrup, chirrup!' shouted all the excited sparrows at once, and each began to yell out what he wanted – red head, yellow beak, green chest, pink wings, white tail and the rest. Really, you never in your life heard such a deafening noise!

Dabble the elf was having a snooze on her bed. She woke up in a hurry and wondered what the dreadful noise was. She opened her window and looked out. Her garden was full of screeching sparrows, pecking at one another and stirring up the dust.

'Be quiet!' said Dabble.

'Chirrup, chirrup, chirrup,' screamed the sparrows. Then they caught sight of Dabble and shouted at her loudly, 'We want to ask you to give us something that will make us look different from the hen sparrows –

blue legs, or pink wings – or something.'

'Oh, I'll give you something, all right!' said Dabble crossly. 'Come in, one by one.'

So the sparrows went in one by one at her front door – and were pushed out one by one at her back door – and when they came out they were wearing little black bibs under their chins! Yes, every one of them!

'*Babies!* Quarrelsome *babies*, that's all you are!' said Dabble, shutting the door on the last one. 'And babies wear bibs – so you can wear them too!'

And it's a funny thing, but since that day every cock sparrow has to wear a black bib under his chin in the springtime. You look and see!

Where Shall We Nest?

Where Shall We Nest?

ONCE UPON a time all the birds had a meeting. The big rook took the topmost bough, and began the talking.

'*Caw-caw!* This meeting is held to find out which would be the best places for us to nest in this year. Last year so many boys and girls found our nests and eggs, and alas! Some of them took the eggs.'

'So we must try to find safer places to build in,' said the freckled thrush. 'Safe places, safer places!'

'*Tirry-lee,*' said the red robin, his bold black eyes looking all around. 'The very best places to build in are old kettles, or saucepans, or old boots in a ditch.

Anything that has belonged to man is nice to build in.'

'I don't think so,' said the blue tit. 'But you are so friendly to man, aren't you, robin? You are not afraid of him as we are. No kettles for me! I always think some sort of a hole is the safest place.'

'Well, you built in somebody's letter box last year,' said the thrush. 'That belonged to man, didn't it?'

'Well, it was a nice *hole*,' said the blue tit. 'I chose it because it was a hole, not because it had anything to do with man.'

'Holes in trees are best,' said the great tit.

The woodpecker nodded his red-splashed head. 'Yes, holes are good,' he said.

'There aren't enough holes,' said the starling. 'It's all very well for the woodpecker to talk – he can always *make* holes by drumming with his beak into the wood. We can't!'

'I think that the very best place is just under the eaves of a house,' said the little house martin. 'It's cosy there, and the eaves protect the nest.'

'What! Build a nest so near to people!' said the rook. '*Caw-caw!* You must be mad. Don't the rough boys come and tear down your nests? *I* like to build in the topmost branches of high trees, right away from man.'

'Well, you sometimes spoil his corn for him,' said the robin. 'So he likes to shoot you, and you have to get far away from him when you build.'

'If the summer is going to be fine, with few storms, we like to build our big nests high in the topmost boughs,' said the rook. 'But if the summer is going to be stormy, we build in the lower ones. We are very clever.'

'Yes, that *is* clever,' said the blackbird. 'High-built nests would be torn away by the wind during a storm. You are wise, rook. But all the same, I say that the best place for a nest is somewhere close-hidden in a tree like the oak or the chestnut, or in a close-set hedge.'

'Too easily found,' said a big gull, soaring round. 'If you take *my* advice, you will build somewhere on high cliffs where it is difficult for people to get to your nests.'

'We don't all live by the sea,' said the moorhen. 'If you will let me say a word, I advise everyone to find a nice quiet pond, go to some rushes, and build a nest there. You can so easily bend down the rushes, and make a sort of platform nest. Then, when you leave your nest, you can bend rushes over it to hide it.'

'A good idea,' said the jackdaw. 'But I should be afraid of my little ones falling into the water. It's all right for *you*, moorhen, because you can swim. But jackdaws can't.'

'You build in queer places,' said the kingfisher, looking at the big jackdaw. 'Who else would choose a church tower! Why, it must take you ages and ages to build a nest there, because you have to fill it up with sticks!'

'Well, who would want to build a nest like you, tucked into a long hole in a bank!' said the jackdaw. 'Nasty and dark and smelly!'

'The sand martin builds in holes in banks too,' said the kingfisher. 'And it's a very good idea, isn't it, sand martin?'

'Very good,' said the little brown sand martin. 'We sand martins like to build our nests all together, you know. I build mine in the sandy bank of an old quarry. I make a hole in it, and lay my eggs at the end of it.'

'Supposing rain came, and soaked down into the sandbank, and got into your hole,' said the starling. 'Your babies would be drowned.'

'No, they wouldn't,' said the sand martin at once. '*I* make my hole slant *up*wards – so any water always runs down and out!'

'That is a good idea,' said the starling. 'Well, has anyone any more to say? We still haven't decided what is the best place to nest.'

Everyone said what he thought, but they couldn't agree. Those that built in holes meant to go on building in holes. Those that built in trees would not change. So they began to talk about what were the best things to use in the building of a nest.

'Maybe we can choose something that no one will notice,' said the rook. '*I* think big twigs are the best.'

'Oh, *no*,' said the blue tit. 'I should hate a nest made of big twigs. Moss and root fibres and feathers – that is the sort of thing you want.'

'I prefer a mud nest,' said the house martin firmly, and the barn swallow nodded too. 'Mud makes a fine firm nest.'

'It must be difficult to make,' said the lark in surprise. 'I don't bother much about making a wonderful nest. The print of a horse's foot in a field is a good enough place for me to nest in, and just a few bits of grass.'

'Mud makes a wonderful nest,' said the house martin. 'You fly down to a puddle, and take some mud in your beak like this, and mix a bit of straw with it—'

But nobody wanted to hear. The kingfisher began

to talk loudly. '*Kee, kee, kee!* Listen to me! *I* make a very fine nest, and all I use is – fish bones!'

'*Fish* bones!' said the birds in surprise. 'How queer! Don't they smell horrid?'

'Yes, they do, but we don't notice it,' said the kingfisher. 'You see, my mate and I catch plenty of fish, and we use the old bones for a nest, putting them in a pile. They make a fine nest, really they do.'

'Well, we don't all want to catch fish in order to make a nasty, smelly nest of fish bones,' said the thrush rather rudely. 'I like a nice firm nest made of small twigs, roots, moss, and things like that. And I like a mud lining.'

'So do I,' said the blackbird, 'but I do like a nice soft lining on top of the mud. I can never understand why you don't put one on, thrush.'

'No need to,' said the thrush, 'no need to, no need to, no need to!'

'I always think it is best to make my nest of something near at hand,' said the robin. 'For instance, I usually build my nest somewhere near the ground, where there are plenty of dead leaves lying about. Very well – if I use dead leaves, my nest can hardly be seen; it is just a mass of dead leaves, among other dead leaves!'

'Quite good,' said the chaffinch, thinking of her own neat and pretty little nest. 'Linings are very important too, I always think. I like a soft, warm lining for my eggs. Warmth is a good thing for eggs.'

'Oh, I think so too!' said the long-tailed tit eagerly. 'You should feel how warm *my* nest is, when it's finished. I use feathers inside it – hundreds of them, really hundreds!'

'Well, it isn't everyone that can spare the time to go hunting for as many feathers as *you* use!' said the robin. 'I shouldn't be surprised if you put over a thousand feathers inside your ball of a nest. It must be so hot inside that I wonder your eggs aren't cooked!'

There was a silence. All the birds looked at one another, for they were longing to fly off and begin to make their nests. But nothing had been decided!

'Well,' said the rook at last, 'shall we all build high up in tall trees, as I do?'

'No, in *holes*!' cried the tits, the starlings, the woodpeckers, the kingfishers and the sand martins.

'No, on the ground,' called the larks, the plovers and the robins.

'No, in barns!' cried the barn swallows. '*We* always build in barns.'

'No, under the eaves!' cried the house martins.

There was a great noise of twittering and singing, and no one could really make out what was being said. A big bird suddenly flew down, cocked his head on one side, and said, 'Cuckoo! Cuckoo!'

'Oh, you didn't come to the meeting!' cried the birds. 'You haven't said what *you* think! What is the best place to nest, cuckoo, and what are the best things to use for a nest?'

'The best place to nest is nowhere!' cried the cuckoo, 'and the best things to use are nothing! *I* never make a nest – I use *yours*! Cuckoo! Cuckoo! Fancy asking *me*!'

He flew off – and so did everyone else. And if you look and see this year, you will find that each bird has chosen the place *he* thinks the best, and is using what *he* likes most for his nest. It's really fun to watch them so busily at work!

Betty and the Lambs' Tails

'Betty and the Lambs' Tails

ALL THE children liked nature lessons. It was fun to hear about the animals and birds and flowers. They liked hunting for things in the hedges and trees, in the fields and woods.

Miss Wills, the teacher, had made a big nature chart, which she put on the wall. There was a space left for every day.

'Now,' she said, 'I want *someone* to fill in every space!'

'How can we?' asked Jack.

'Well,' said Miss Wills, 'any boy or girl who finds something new or strange or lovely in their walks, can draw it or write a piece about it in the space for that day. And they must put their name in the space too, so that we shall know who gave us that nice piece of nature news.'

'That's a fine idea,' said Betty. 'It will be fun to fill up the spaces, Miss Wills. I hope I get my name there heaps of times.'

'Well, you will have to use your eyes a little more than you do, Betty, if you want your name on the chart,' said Miss Wills. 'You are not very good at noticing things yet!'

'I shall try,' said Betty.

'I know one thing we can look for now, before the leaves grow on the trees,' said Joan. 'We can look for old birds' nests. We shan't be able to find them easily when the trees begin to leaf.'

'And we can look for new flowers, and listen to the birds beginning to sing their spring songs,' said Pat.

It was Pat who filled up the first space on the chart. He found a yellow coltsfoot, a *very* early one!

He proudly drew it on the chart, and then signed his name.

Ellen filled the next space. She saw a lark fly up from the ground, high into the sky, and heard him singing his loud, sweet song. She found a picture, copied it, and then signed her name in the space for that day.

'A flower and a bird already,' said Miss Wills. 'How gay our chart will look when it is finished!'

Harry found a butterfly sleeping in the loft. It was a lovely yellow. 'It is a brimstone,' said Miss Wills. 'Well done, Harry. You can make it a fine bright yellow on the chart. Sign your name – that's right.'

'Betty hasn't put anything on the chart yet,' said Pat. 'She said she was going to find heaps of things. But she never does. Where are your eyes, Betty? You never seem to see *anything*!'

'Oh dear!' said Betty. 'I really will look hard.' So she did. And, on the way to school that morning, as she went down the long lane, she did see something!

She was looking in the hedges for an old nest – and she found a new one!

It was a blackbird's nest, and the blackbird was still making it. It was almost finished, and the blackbird was putting a soft lining of grass on to the mud he had placed at the bottom of his nest.

'Oh – he's actually *making* it!' cried Betty, and she peeped at it to make sure it really was a new one. There it was, set firmly in the fork of a little tree. The tree grew higher than the hedge, and was covered with long catkins that shook in the breeze. The wind blew, and yellow pollen powder flew from the catkins all over Betty's head.

'I shall have my name on the chart! I shall draw the nest!' cried Betty. She rushed off to school and told Miss Wills.

'I must go and see if it really *is* a blackbird's nest,' said Miss Wills. 'If it is a new one, we mustn't disturb the bird too much or it will fly away and not lay its eggs there.'

Miss Wills, Betty and Jack all went to see if the nest was really a blackbird's. And will you believe it, Betty couldn't find the nest! They hunted up the hedge and down the hedge, but they couldn't find the nest.

'It was well hidden,' said Betty. 'Oh, Miss Wills, can't I count it? Can't I put it on the chart?'

'I'm afraid I must see it,' said Miss Wills. 'Now we really must go back, Betty. It's late.'

Betty was sad. They went back to school, and on the way there Jack kept looking at Betty's dark hair. He wondered what the yellow powder was, scattered all over it.

And he suddenly knew. 'Of course! It's from the lambs' tail catkins growing in the hedge! Betty must have leant over to look at the nest, and the hazel tree shook its pollen powder all over her. Now, if I can find a hazel tree with catkins in the lane, all I have to do is to look in the lower branches for the nest!'

On the way home Jack looked for a hazel tree with

catkins. There were two or three growing out of the hedge beside the lane. He looked carefully into the hedge below the trees for a nest.

And he found the blackbird's nest under one of the trees! Above his head the wind shook the lambs' tails, and yellow pollen powder blew all over Jack's head, just as it had blown over Betty's.

That afternoon Jack took Miss Wills to the nest. 'How did you know where to look for it this time?' asked Miss Wills.

Jack told her, 'The nut tree told me! The yellow pollen from the hazel tree's catkins was all over Betty's hair – so I knew she must have found a nest just below a hazel!'

'Clever boy,' said Miss Wills. 'I think you will have to count the nest as yours, but Betty can sign her name in the space too. A little share of it must be hers, as she first found the nest.'

Betty was sad when she heard that she could not count the nest as hers. 'I am silly not to have noticed where it was,' she said. 'I do think you are clever, Jack, to have seen the yellow stuff on my hair. I wonder why the hazel tree sends out such a lot of powder.'

She went to have a look at the hazel tree on the way home. 'How queer that you should make such a lot of pollen powder in your long catkins!' she said to the tree. The wind blew, and the catkins shook and danced like long tails. Clouds of yellow powder flew out.

'What a waste!' said Betty. 'I wonder why you make that yellow pollen powder? Is it to help to make nuts for us, I wonder?'

The little girl began to look carefully at the bare brown hazel twigs. She saw some tiny buds growing on them – and then, much to her surprise, she saw that some of the buds had tiny red spikes hanging out of the middle of them.

'That's queer!' said Betty to herself. 'That's very queer! Why do some of these little buds have red spikes? Are they a kind of flower bud?'

She picked two or three twigs with buds on. She took them to school with her, and showed them to Miss Wills.

'Look, Miss Wills,' she said. 'I went to have a peep at the blackbird's nest under the boughs of the hazel tree, and I noticed that some of the hazel buds have these funny red spikes hanging out. What are they?'

'Dear me, Betty *has* begun to use her eyes well!' said Miss Wills, pleased. 'Betty, the hazel tree grows two kinds of flowers – the pollen flowers, which are the lambs' tails we love so much – and these funny little red-spike flowers.'

'What are they for?' asked Betty.

'They make the nuts that we like to pick in the autumn,' said Miss Wills. 'As soon as some of the yellow pollen powder flies to these red spikes, they can begin to make nuts. I *am* glad you saw them, Betty.'

'Can I draw the catkins and the red-spike buds on the chart, and sign my name there?' asked Betty.

'Of course!' said Miss Wills. 'It is one of the best things we shall have down for this month, Betty. Well done!'

Betty was very proud. She drew the catkins on the chart, and she drew and coloured some of the little buds that had red spikes. She drew a few that hadn't too.

'They are leaf buds,' said Miss Wills. 'You have three things there, Betty, haven't you – the pollen catkins, the nut flowers and the leaf buds? That is really very good.'

'I shall watch the nut buds and see how the nuts grow,' said Betty. 'Isn't it funny, Miss Wills? The blackbird's nest made me see something else! It's fun to find something all by myself.'

Betty is watching the nut buds of the hazel tree. Can *you* find the catkins and the red-spike buds, and watch the nuts growing too?

The Cross Little
Tadpole

The Cross Little Tadpole

ONCE UPON a time a big mass of jelly lay on the top of a pond. In it were tiny black specks, like little black commas.

The sun shone down and warmed the jelly. A fish tried to nibble a bit, but it was too slippery. A big black beetle tried a little too, but he didn't like it. The rain came and pattered down on the jelly.

Every day the tiny black specks grew bigger. They were eggs. Soon it would be time for them to hatch, and swim about as tadpoles in the pond.

The day came when the black eggs had become wriggling tadpoles, and then the jelly began to disappear. It was no longer needed. It had saved the eggs from being eaten, because it was too slippery for any creature to gobble up for its dinner. It had helped to hold the eggs up to the sunshine too. But now it was of no more use.

The little black wrigglers swam to a water weed and held on to it. They were very tiny. When they were hungry they nibbled the weed. It tasted nice to them.

They grew bigger each day in the pond, and soon the other creatures began to know them. 'There go two tadpoles!' said the stickleback, all his spines standing up along his back.

'Funny creatures, aren't they?' said the big black beetle. 'All head and tail – nothing much else to them!'

'Hundreds of them!' said the water snail. 'The whole pond is full of them.'

'I like them for my dinner,' said the dragonfly grub. 'Look – I hide down here in the mud, and when I see a nice fat tadpole swimming by, out I pounce and catch one in my jaw.'

A good many of the tadpoles were eaten by enemies,

because they were not sharp enough or fast enough to escape. Those that were left grew big, and raced about the pond, wriggling their long tails swiftly.

One little tadpole had some narrow escapes. One of the black beetles nearly caught him – in fact, a tiny piece was bitten off his tail. Another time he scraped himself badly on the spines of the stickleback.

And twice the dragonfly grub darted at him and almost caught him. Each time the little tadpole was very cross.

'Leave me alone! What harm am I doing to you? I don't want to be your dinner!'

The pond had other things in it besides the fish, the grubs and the beetles. It had some frogs, and the little tadpole was always in a temper about these.

'Those big, fat frogs are so rude and bad-mannered,' he said to the other tadpoles. 'How I hate them with their gaping mouths and great big eyes!'

The frogs didn't like the cross little tadpole because he called rude names after them. Sometimes they chased him, swimming fast with their strong hind legs.

'If once we catch you, we shall make you sorry!' they croaked.

The tadpole swam behind a stone and called back to them, 'Old croakers! Old greedy-mouths! Old stick-out eyes!'

The frogs tried to overturn the stone and get at the rude tadpole. But he burrowed down in the mud, and came up far behind them.

'Old croakers!' he cried. 'Here I am – peep-bo! Old croakers!'

The frogs lay in wait for the rude tadpole. He never knew when a fat green frog would jump into the water from the bank, almost on top of him. He never knew when one would scramble out of the mud just below him.

'I'm tired of these frogs,' he told the other tadpoles. 'I wish somebody would eat them. I wish those ducks would come back and gobble them up!'

The tadpole had never forgotten one day when some wild ducks had flown down to the pond, and had frightened all the frogs and other creatures very much indeed.

The ducks had caught and eaten three frogs and at least twenty tadpoles. It had been a dreadful day. None of the tadpoles ever forgot it.

'You shouldn't wish for those ducks to come back!' said the stickleback. '*You* might be eaten yourself!'

'I'm getting too big to be eaten,' said the cross tadpole. 'Stickleback, what else eats frogs?'

'The grass snake eats frogs,' said the pretty little stickleback. 'I once saw him come sliding down into the water. He swam beautifully. He ate four frogs when he came.'

'I've a good mind to go and tell him to come to this pond and eat some more frogs,' said the tadpole. 'He might be glad to know there was a good meal here for him.'

'Well, he is lying in the sun on the bank of the pond,

over there,' said the stickleback. 'Go and tell him now! But, tadpole – listen to me – I don't think I have ever met anyone quite so silly as you in all my life!'

'Pooh!' said the tadpole rudely, and swam off towards the bank on which the long grass snake was lying, curled up in a heap.

The tadpole poked his black head out of the water and called to the snake, 'Hi, grass snake! Can you hear me?'

The snake woke up in surprise. He looked at the tadpole. 'What do you want?' he said.

'I've come to tell you that there are a lot of horrid, nasty frogs in this pond, that would make a very good dinner for you,' said the tadpole. 'If you slide into the water now I'll show you where to look for them. I'd be glad if you would eat every frog you can see, because they lie in wait for me and try to catch me.'

The snake put out his quivering tongue and then drew it in again. 'I would come today, but I have just had a very good meal,' he said. 'I will come back some day when I am hungry, and you shall show me where to find the frogs then.'

He glided off through the grass. The tadpole swam back to his friends in excitement.

'What do you think?' he cried. 'I've told the grass snake about those horrid frogs! He is coming back to eat them one day soon!'

The days went on, warm, sunny days. The tadpole grew and grew. One day he noticed that he had two back legs, and he was most astonished.

'Hallo!' he said. 'I've got legs! So have all the other tadpoles. Rather nice!'

Then he noticed that he had front legs as well. His tail became shorter. He wanted to breathe up in the air, instead of breathing down in the water.

He and the other tadpoles found a little bit of wood on the surface of the water, and they climbed up on to it. It was nice to sit there in the sunshine, breathing the warm air. It was fun to flick out a little tongue to see if any fly could be caught by it.

'This is a nice life!' said the cross tadpole. 'A very nice life. I like living in this warm pond. Most of those horrid frogs have gone now, so life is very pleasant.'

'There's your friend, the grass snake,' said the stickleback, poking his head up suddenly. 'Why don't you go and tell him to come and gobble up all the frogs in this pond, as you said you would?'

The tadpole was just about to leap off his bit of wood, when he caught sight of himself in the water. The pond was calm that day, like a mirror, and the tadpole could see himself well.

He stared down at himself in horror and amazement – for he did not see a tadpole, but a small frog!

'I've turned into a frog!' he croaked. 'I have, I have! And all the other tadpoles are little frogs too! Why didn't I notice that before?'

'Tadpoles always turn into frogs. I could have told you that before, but you never would listen to anyone,' said the stickleback. 'Well, are you going to find the grass snake and tell him to come and eat you and all your friends too? You said you would tell him where the frogs were in this pond.'

But the tiny frog did not go to tell the snake anything. He felt quite certain that he would be eaten at once. He jumped into the pond with a splash, and swam as fast as he could to the other side of the water.

Wasn't he a silly fellow? He is five years old now, and quite grown-up – but you have only to say 'Snake!' to him to send him leaping away in fright!

The Bumblebee Hums

The Bumblebee Hums

ALL THE hedgerow folk liked to hear the humming of the bees. It was a summery sound, lazy and warm. The earliest bees had been abroad in March, seeking for the flowers that opened on the bank below. More bees had come in April, and very soon there had been heard the loud booming of the big brown and yellow bumblebee. She *did* make a noise. *Zooooooooom! Zooooooooom!* It was a lovely droning sound, never heard in the cold days of winter.

The bumblebee had slept all through the winter in a little hole on the north side of the hedgerow bank. It was a cold hole, full of bitterness when the north winds blew in January and February. But the bumblebee had chosen it carefully. She knew that to choose a warm hole on the south side of the hedge would be dangerous. The sun came early to the south bank, and sent its warm beams into every nook and cranny there, waking up all the small sleepers. But to wake up on a sunny day in February and crawl forth might mean death when the frost returned at night. It was best to sleep in a cold place, unwarmed by the early sunshine of the year, and not to wake until all fear of frosts was past.

The bumblebee had carefully made a honeypot for herself before going to sleep. Then, if by chance she should awake, she could have a sip of honey from her pot and need not run the risk of leaving her hole. The hole was small. It had been made by a worm, and the bee squatted down in the enlarged room at the end of the hole, her honeypot beside her. She did not wake until February, and then although the sun was shining warmly on the south side of the hedge, her hole was still rimmed round by frost and she did not stir out. She sipped her honey and went to sleep again.

At last, on a warm spring day, she walked out, feeling rather top-heavy and a little dazed with her long, cold sleep. She spread her wings and the hedgerow heard once again the loud booming hum that it liked so much in the summertime. The warm days must be coming if the bumblebee was about!

The bee decided to look for a new hole – a warm one this time, and a bigger one. She knew the hedgerow well, and thought it would be good to find one there, for then she would not need to learn new surroundings. So she began her hunt.

There was one rather big hole on the south side, but the bumblebee came out quickly after one look, for a most enormous spider lived there! She looked under an old stone and saw a fat toad peering at her with gleaming eyes. He knew she was dangerous and did not flick out his tongue to eat her. She backed out quickly. Then she flew to another part of the bank, humming busily, enjoying herself in the hot sun. And at last she found exactly the right hole!

It had been made by mice, and their smell still hung about the little hole. The bumblebee altered the hole to her liking and then fetched in some moss. She crawled out again and brought back some grass. Then she visited some flowers and returned with pollen which she packed into the hole. She looked at the heap of moss, grass and pollen, and decided it was time to lay her eggs.

So she built some egg cells and put pollen into each. Then she laid her eggs, one in each cell – white long-shaped eggs that she loved very much. She spread herself over them to brood them. By her were several of her honeypots, full of honey. She was glad when her eggs hatched out into grubs – but how hungry they were! They soon ate up all the pollen in their cells, and the bumblebee knew they were hungry. So in each cell she bit a tiny hole, and passed more food through to her growing children.

Now the big bumblebee was busy all day long. She went out to find food for her first batch of children; she laid more eggs; she built more and more cells; she taught the first batch of young bees how to help her. She was happy, and the hedgerow liked to hear her going booming about her work.

One morning she heard the loud humming of another creature nearby, and she stopped in her flight to see who it was. It was a large queen wasp, and the bumblebee was interested to see that she was doing exactly what she herself had done some weeks before – she was hunting for a hole in the bank!

'You are late in finding a home,' boomed the big bumblebee.

'I only awake when the sun has plenty of warmth in it,' buzzed the wasp. 'All the winter I slept in a hidden cranny behind an ivy root in the hedge. A little mouse once woke me up when he came hunting for the nuts the squirrel hid, but he soon fled when he saw *me*!'

'*I* have a fine nest in an old mouse hole,' hummed

the bee, settling down beside the big queen wasp. 'Come and see it.'

But the wasp was in a hurry. She was anxious to find a hole for herself and begin her building. The summer would soon be here and she must lay her eggs. She ran to a hole and crawled inside to see if it would suit her. But a big beetle was there, and showed her his great, ugly jaws. The wasp hurried out again and flew to another hole. This was too big, and full of rubbish.

At last she found exactly what she needed. This was an old tunnel made by the mole the summer before. Part of the roof had fallen in at the back. The wasp walked all over the hole, touching the walls with her feelers. This was a good place. She was pleased with it. She crawled up to the roof and found there the root of a hawthorn bush jutting out. She could hang her nest from that.

She left the hole and flew up into the air, circling round as she did so, noticing everything around her hole – the stone nearby, the tuft of grass, the thistle

– all these things would help her to know her hole again. Then she flew higher still into the air, and noticed bigger things – the nearby ditch, the hedgerow itself, the big bramble spray that waved high in the air. Ah, she would know her way back again now!

The queen wasp was going to build a city and be its ruler. She was going to have thousands of subjects, who would work for her night and day. She was longing to begin, for the warm sun had heated her blood and given her strength and joy.

She flew off to the common up on the hill, and looked about her as she went. She was hunting for a piece of oak from which she could take a scraping to start her city. She found a gatepost and settled down on it. She bit a piece of wood out, a mere shaving, with her strong jaws. She chewed it and chewed it until it was paper pulp. Then back she flew to the hole she had taken for her own. She crawled in – and immediately began a fierce buzzing, for there were three ants there! She drove her sting into each one and threw them out of the hole, little curled-up brown things, poisoned by her sting.

She stuck the paper pellet to the root at the top of the hole and then went off for more. In and out she flew all day long, building the roof of her house first, for the wasp people live in topsy-turvy homes! Every time she left the hole she carried with her a pellet of earth, for she wanted to have plenty of room for her city.

She often met the big bumblebee, who told her that she had now plenty of workers to help her, for many of her grubs had grown into bees, and did her work.

'Come and play for a while,' said the bumblebee. 'The fields are full of flowers.'

'I have no use for flowers,' said the wasp impatiently. 'Leave me, cousin. I am too busy. I have many things to do, and I have as yet no helpers as you have! What there is to be done I do myself.'

Soon there was a pile of earth outside the old mole hole, and inside, built safely under an umbrella-like covering of grey paper, were many wasp cells, each containing a small grub. They hung head downwards in their cells, and were tightly glued to the top so that they could not fall out of the hole at the bottom. Soon they grew large and fat, and were so wedged in that they could not have fallen out if they had wanted to.

Then each grub spun a silk sheet over the cell opening and formed a cocoon. The queen wasp waited impatiently for them to come forth from their cells, and at last the time came. Each little wasp bit through its cell and came out. They cleaned themselves up, and then looked round the nest. Very soon they were helping the queen wasp, their mother, to do the tasks she had done for some weeks alone.

They helped to feed the new grubs. They cleaned the nest – and then one morning, when the sun came right into the hole, the young wasps went to the opening and looked out. What a glorious world of light and warmth! They spread out their shining wings and flew into the air, each small wasp taking careful notice of all the things around their hole so that they would know the way back, and would not get lost. Then off they went, all knowing exactly what to do, although they had never done their new tasks before.

Some of them found the old oak post from which their mother had scraped shavings to make the paper-pulp she used in building her city. They too took scrapings and chewed them into pulp, taking the pellets home again to build on to their nest, which was now three storeys high. Other wasps went to a sunny wall on which many flies crawled. They caught the flies, cut off their wings, heads and legs, and carried them back to the nest to feed the young grubs. One wasp found a hiding place in which four moths crouched and, cutting off their wings, carried the bodies away for food. They were all busy, all happy.

They had their enemies, and so had the young bumblebees, who were also helping their mother in the nest. The spotted flycatcher had come back from its winter haunts and darted at the passing bees and wasps, as well as at the flies. Even the queen wasp herself had a narrow escape one day. The great tit too would sometimes wait outside the hole where the bumblebee had her nest, and would pounce on an unwary bee just leaving.

One day all the bees and the wasps heard a strange noise. It was a high humming, very shrill and loud, like a wasp or bee army on the march. Every wasp and every bumblebee flew to see what it was – and they saw a strange sight! A great cloud of honeybees was coming over the field towards the hedgerow. It was led by the queen bee, and thousands of bees were following her. The queen wasp flew near and demanded to know what had happened, for she was excited and half frightened by the tremendous humming.

'We come from a hive far away,' boomed the queen honeybee. 'I had so many worker bees that the hive became too small. So I have brought half the hive away with me and I am looking for a new home. I have left behind me some princesses in the hive. One of them will become queen in my place.'

'*We* do not swarm!' said the queen wasp. 'I make my city as big as I want it.'

'You are only a wasp!' buzzed the honeybee. 'Your city will crumble to nothing in the autumn; all your people will die! But my people live with me, for we store up honey for the cold days!'

The wasp shivered. She thought of the days to come when the frost would creep on her again – when her people would freeze and die – her beautiful city eaten by hungry mice! But what did she care? *She* would live! Next spring she would come forth again and once more build a marvellous city. She buzzed happily and flew off to her hole. The swarm settled on the lowest branch of the oak tree, and then in a short while flew off again, no one knew where.

'*Zooooooooom!*' buzzed the bumblebee to the queen wasp. 'Who would be a hive bee and live in slavery? Not I! Give me a hole in a bank and let me be my own mistress! *Zooooooooom!*'

Rabbity Ways

Rabbity Ways

THE NIGHT had been very dark, for there was no moon. Now there was a grey light creeping into the eastern sky.

Daybreak was near. Soon the owls would go home and the bats would fly back to the old barn to sleep. The oak tree that grew out of the hedgerow rustled its leaves in the chilly wind. It was a wise old tree, friendly to all creatures, and loved by a great many.

The hedgerow was old too. In it grew hawthorn, whose leaves were out early in the springtime, green fingers held up to the sun. Bramble sprays flung long arms here and there, as prickly as the wild rose that forced its way up to the sun. Ivy covered one part of the hedge, and here, in blossom time, feasted the last late flies and many beautiful red admirals.

Below was a sunny bank, for the hedgerow faced south. In summertime the birds found wild strawberries on this bank, and the primroses sometimes flowered there in the early days of January. In the ditch below there was moss growing, soft as velvet, and a few graceful ferns. It was always damp there and cool.

Near the old oak tree was a small pond, ringed round with rushes and meadowsweet. Many creatures came to drink there – from the sly red fox down to the striped yellow wasp! All the creatures in the fields around knew the pond well, and often the swallows would come and skim above it, looking for flies.

The hedgerow was in a deserted corner of the field. Nobody came there, not even the children hunting for blackberries. The farmer had forgotten to cut the hedge for years, and it had grown tall and tangled.

Sometimes the wind would bring the sound of the farmer's voice, shouting to his horses in a distant field, but usually the hedgerow knew nothing but the sound of the wind, of bird calls and pattering paws.

Many, many things had happened in and around the hedgerow. The oak tree had rustled its leaves over thousands of insects, birds and animals. Its twigs knew the difference between a squirrel's scampering paws and a bird's light hold. Its acorns had been stolen by all kinds of mice, and by the screeching jays and the hungry nuthatch.

Now it stood whispering in the cool wind of daybreak. Summer was passing over, and soon the oak leaves would lose their dark green hue and would turn brown.

The grey light in the sky became brighter. Beneath the oak tree, where the bank showed a sandy streak, a hole could just be seen. It was a rabbit's burrow. The burrow went down among the roots of the tree, exactly the size of a rabbit's body except now and again when it widened out to make passing places for two meeting rabbits. The tunnel branched off into two or three different burrows, but the rabbits had learnt every foot of them, and always knew which tunnel to take when they wanted to go to the gorse bush, to the bank or to the other side of the pond.

Out of the hole in the bank a rabbit's head appeared. Her big eyes looked through the dim grey light, her nose twitched as she sniffed the air, and her big ears listened to every sound. She wanted to go out and feed on the grass, and she had with her a young family of five rabbits, who were just getting old enough to look after themselves.

'It is safe,' she said to her young ones. 'We can go out. There is no stoat about, and the owls have all gone home.'

They trooped out of the hole. Other rabbits were in the field too, big ones and little ones, for there were many burrows there.

'Keep near the burrow,' said the mother rabbit.

'Then you will not have far to run if danger comes. I am going along the hedgerow. There is a young furze bush there and I shall feed on the juicy shoots. Keep an eye on the other rabbits, and if you see them turn so that their white bobtail shows plainly, dart into your burrow. Bobbing tails mean danger somewhere! And keep your ears pricked too – for if one of the old rabbits scents danger he will drum on the ground with his hind foot to warn us all. Then you must run as fast as you can.'

The little rabbits began to nibble the grass. They felt quite sure they could look after themselves. Their mother ran silently along the hedgerow. Suddenly she stopped and stood so still that it seemed as if she had frozen stiff. She had seen another animal coming through the hedge. It was a brown hare. As soon as the rabbit saw that it was a harmless creature, she ran on towards it. 'You scared me, cousin hare,' she said. 'Is your burrow round here?'

'Burrow!' said the hare, looking in surprise at the

rabbit, her soft eyes gleaming in the grey light. 'I have no burrow. I live above the ground.'

'But how dangerous!' said the rabbit in alarm. 'Stoats and weasels could easily find you! Do you make a nest like the birds?'

'Come with me,' said the hare. 'I will show you where I live. My home is called a form, because it is simply a dent in the ground the size and form of my body. I make it the shape of my body by lying in it, you see. I like to live alone. I should not like to live with others, as you do.'

'But it is safer,' said the rabbit, going with the hare over the field. 'I have left my young ones with the other rabbits, and they will warn them if danger is near. There is safety in numbers.'

'My ears and my nose make me safe,' said the hare. 'I can smell faraway things and hear the slightest noise. Look at my ears. They are longer than yours, cousin. See the black tips too. You have no black tips. Look at my hind legs. Yours are strong, but mine are much stronger. I can run like the w

Suddenly the hare gave a great leap,
many feet over the field. The rabbit was start
the hare called to her.

'Here is my form. I always jump like that before I
go to it, so that I break my trail. Then if weasel or stoat
come round they cannot follow my scent, for it breaks
where I jump! Come here, cousin. I have some young
ones to show you. They are only a few days old.'

The rabbit went to the hare's form. Near it were
other small holes, and in each lay a young hare, a
leveret, its eyes wide open, its body warmly covered
with fur.

'They have made forms of their own,' said the
hare proudly. 'Even when they are young they like to
live alone.'

'My young ones were not like this,' said the rabbit
in surprise, looking at the leverets. 'My children were
born blind and deaf and had no fur on them at all. I
made a special burrow for them, and blocked up the

…ndi…

…and jumped

…led, but

…hould not think

…this. It is a good

…to see and hear, or

…n enemy!'

…he hare. 'Now take me

…would like to see your

young.

The two anim… …ck to the hedgerow. The hare gave another great leap when she left her form. It was a favourite trick of hers not only when leaving her home, but when she was hunted by dogs. Sometimes she would double on her tracks too, to throw off her hunters. It nearly always deceived them.

The hare was astonished to see the burrow in which the rabbits lived. 'But how do you manage about your ears?' she asked. 'Do you bend them back when you run underground? That must be very uncomfortable. It is a strange idea to tunnel in the earth. I am sure that our family were not meant to do so, or we would not have been given such long ears. It must be difficult too, to dig out all the earth.'

'No, it is easy,' said the rabbit, 'I dig with my front paws and shovel out the earth with my hind paws. See, cousin, there are my children feeding over there.'

The hare was looking at the young rabbits in the light of the dawn when a curious noise came to her long ears. It was a drumming sound, and it seemed to the hare as if the ground were quivering under her feet. The mother rabbit called to her young ones at once.

'Come here! There is danger about! That is the old rabbit drumming with his hind feet to warn us. Come, cousin, you must hide in our burrow too.'

The young rabbits lifted their heads when they heard the drumming. Then they saw all the other rabbits running in every direction to their holes, their white bobtails showing clearly. In seconds the young ones were off too, scampering to their hole. Not a rabbit was to be seen when the old red fox came slinking by. The hare had gone too – but not down the burrow.

My legs are safer than a burrow! she thought to herself. *I shall run, not hide! No fox can catch* me*!*

Poor hare! thought the rabbit. *She ought to dig a burrow, then she would be safe. The fox will surely get her.*

But the fox went hungry that morning!

The Whistler

The Whistler

IN THE lovely month of May the hedgerow was beautiful to see. The hawthorn leaves were a brilliant green, the brambles threw graceful branches into the air, full of tender young leaves, and the ivy shone dark and glossy. When the may blossom came it lay along the hedgerow like drifts of summer snow, and its fragrance brought a myriad bees, moths, butterflies and other insects to it. The hedgerow animals smelt it too, and rejoiced because it was a summer smell – a smell belonging to warm days and happy times.

The oak tree was now full of leaf. It was the last of all the trees to put out its tender feather-shaped leaves, and the birds whose nests were among its branches were glad of their shelter. They liked the soft green light that the leaves made, and they liked to see them waving in the wind. It was good to have a nest in the oak tree in May.

On the bank below there were many flowers, glad of the hot sun. The cow parsley foamed there, and in the wet ditch great clumps of golden kingcups raised their heads to the sun. Lilac milkmaids, the pretty cuckoo flower, grew in the field and danced gaily all day long. Buttercups made a carpet of gold, and red clover raised its sweet head to the humming bees. All day long the cuckoo called. It never seemed to stop. It was a summer sound and the hedgerow folk liked it.

At sunset, when the buttercups glowed even more golden, and the shadow of the oak tree was long, so long that it stretched halfway across the field, a strange sound was heard. It was a clear low whistle, rather bird-like. It came from the pond that lay not far from the oak tree. The hedgerow folk heard it, and knew what it was.

It was the otter whistling to his mate. She lived in the pond, for it was very deep in places, and big fish could be found there. It had once been part of a stream that had run into the river not far away, but the stream had been altered in its course so that it emptied itself into the river at a different place – and the big pond was all that was left of the old part of the stream.

In the old days many otters had swum in the pond when it had been part of the stream, and even now, when it was only a pond, they came to it, travelling over the fields. It had the alder trees they loved, and beneath the roots of the alders were fine hiding places, holes where an otter could rest in peace, well hidden from all eyes. It was a good pond.

In the autumn before, two otters had come to the pond. The hedgerow knew them well, both in the water and out. The birds knew the least about them, for the otters were night-time creatures, and most birds sleep through the night. The owl knew them best, and sometimes hooted to them when he heard the otters whistling to one another.

The otters were dusky-brown creatures covered with dense fur – so thick that not a drop of water could wet their warm bodies. They were large creatures, about four feet long. The inquisitive hedgehog often sniffed at the 'spur' of footprint left by the otters in the mud at the side of the pond. These prints showed the otters to have rounded toes, webbed for swimming, for they were marvellous swimmers.

Sometimes at sunset the late robin could see two flat black heads moving about on the pond surface. Then he knew that the otters were astir. He watched them swimming and playing, rolling their oily bodies round in a circle, as clever as fish in the water. They swam with their front paws only, and used their long flattened tails as rudders. It was wonderful to watch them.

The alder trees knew the otters very well indeed,

for had they not made their nursery under their roots? The alders sighed in the wind and remembered. The mother otter had found the big hole one day and had whistled to her mate to come and look. To get to the hole under the roots they had to dive right into the water, and then scramble into the underground chamber as best they could. The hole led upwards, criss-crossed by alder roots. At its top end it was dry and roomy.

'This will do for our nursery,' said the otter to her mate. 'No one will find us here. There will be plenty of room for all of us when the babies come. I shall bring rushes and grass here, and the purple flowers of the great reed, and make a soft nest.'

And that winter, during a warm spell, the mother otter laid her three little ones there in the big dark hole under the alders. They were quite blind, but they were already covered with a warm, downy fur. The mother was very proud of them and licked them all over. So did the father. They smelt sweet, those tiny otters, and were so warm and playful.

'You must hunt for us,' said the mother to her mate. 'It is cold tonight, and I must not leave these little ones to get chilled. Go and bring us some fish. I am hungry.'

The big otter slid into the water. He closed his short, rounded ears all the time he was under the surface so that no water should get into them. He went to the deepest part of the pond where he knew there were big fish, and very soon chased and caught one. Back he went to the hole.

The mother otter bit a large piece out of the fish's shoulder, and then ate the fish all the way down to the tail. This she left, for in the otter family it is not good manners to eat the tail. The tiny otters sniffed and snickered round the little bits of fish the mother had left. The smell excited them.

The alder trees often felt the little otters scrambling about over their roots, and they liked it. And then one evening, when the sun had just gone down, leaving a golden glow in the western sky, the mother otter took her young ones into the pond for the first time. What an adventure for them!

They had often been to the edge of the water that lapped into their dark hole. One of them had even slipped into it, and been pulled out by its mother, who scolded it and bit it sharply for a punishment. But this was the first time they had ever been out into the great world beyond their small, dark home under the alder roots.

'Come!' said the otter to her three young ones. She slid into the water and one by one the three small otters followed her. They did not feel the chill of the water, for by now they had thick, dense fur coats – two coats, really, one of short fur and one of longer hairs.

At first they floundered about, not at all sure what to do in the water – but their mother was patient with them. She took them quickly up to the surface, for she knew they could not at first go very long without breathing. Then she showed them how to swim properly.

'Use your tail to guide you,' she said. 'Use your front paws for swimming. Let your back paws drag loose.'

The young otters were clumsy at first, but they enjoyed the adventure. What a fine place the world was! They watched their mother and father swim gracefully here and there, turning and tumbling easily through the water. They gazed in amazement as they saw a large fish chased and caught, and they snickered together in terror when they spied their mother chasing a startled moorhen, which, taking to its wings, escaped just in time!

All through the springtime the young otters learnt many things from their parents. They learnt how to turn over the big stones to hunt for crayfish. They found out how to twist and turn swiftly in the water to catch a darting fish. They were taken on land and found that they could run easily on their four webbed feet. They caught frogs for themselves, and grew fat and strong.

One night the father otter whistled goodbye to his mate. 'The youngsters are big now,' he said. 'I am going away to the sea.'

'Why is that?' asked his mate.

'This pond is drying up a little,' answered the otter. 'I am afraid that it may disappear altogether if the summer is hot. Even the river nearby may dry up, and as I count on the current to take me down to the sea, I shall go while there is plenty of time. I shall spend the summer in an old sea cave I know, where many bats live. In the autumn I will come back to you.'

The big otter swam to the edge of the pond, shook the water from his thick coat like a dog and disappeared in the long grass. He had gone to the river. The robin, who loved the long twilight evenings of May time, followed him, flitting along the hedgerow beside him. She saw him enter the swiftly flowing river, and, with front paws pressed under his chin, float gently down with the current.

His mate missed him sadly. The hedgerow folk often heard her whistling for him on these warm May evenings when the sunset glow lasted for a long time in the western skies. She wanted him to see what lusty fellows their cubs had grown, she wanted him to swim and play with her on these sweet warm nights. But he had gone.

The weather grew hotter. The pond, never very full since a hot summer two years since, grew lower. The mother otter found that her underground chamber was now hardly under water. It would soon be no longer a safe hiding place. She hunted around the pond for another. But there was none big enough for four otters.

'We must part,' said the mother to her young ones. 'You are old enough to go your own way now. You can fish and swim, dive and walk for miles on the land if need be. You know how to avoid traps. I have taken you to the river and shown you how to let the current carry you along. You have often found holes big enough to hide in. Now the time has come for you to work for yourselves.'

'But where will *you* go?' asked the smallest of the three.

'I may go down to the sea too, as your father did,' said the otter. 'There are many things there to eat that we do not find inland.'

'Is there fish there?' asked the biggest otter hungrily.

'Shoals and shoals!' said his mother. 'I shall come back in the late autumn, maybe to this very pond, and perhaps your father will come too, to find me and play with me as he used to do. Ah, it is good to go up the rivers in the autumn! For then there are many eels coming down to the sea, and they are very good to eat!'

'Goodbye!' whistled the young otters, and they swam away from their mother. One went overland to the stream and swam up it. One went to the hole under the alder roots and lay there, sorrowing to think that the happy family life was broken. And the third went to a marshy place he knew in a withy bed two miles off. The mother otter swam once round the pond she knew so well, and then, whistling clearly, she left it and made her way to the river.

'I shall return in the autumn!' she called to the inquisitive robin. 'Look for me then!'

The Adventurers

.

The Adventurers

OCTOBER DAYS had been sunny and warm, and there were many blackberries ripe in the hedgerow. Some of the bramble leaves were turning scarlet and gold, and glowed brightly when the sun shone through them. The ivy was blooming on the hedge just below the oak tree, and to it came hundreds of bluebottle flies, late butterflies, wasps, bees and little creeping insects. It was the last feast of the year before winter set in.

The swallows and the martins had revelled in the warm October sunshine, but they did not like the chilly nights. The oak tree felt the wind of their wings all day long as they flew around, for many of the insects that fed on the ivy flowers below flew up into the air when they were satisfied, and were chased and caught by the keen-eyed swallows. The martins too knew where the ivy blossom was, with its insects, and darted up and down over the hedge, catching unwary bluebottles as they buzzed noisily over the ivy.

The rabbits, peeping out of their holes, knew the birds well. They had arrived one April morning, when the south wind was blowing strongly, a great crowd of them together, crying, '*Feetafeetit, feetafeetit*' to one another. They were weary little birds then, but very happy. They had flown a long way to come to the fields they knew, for they all wished to nest in the spot they had loved so well the year before.

'There is the oak tree!' they cried to one another as they circled round it. 'And see, here is the hedgerow where the ivy blooms later on! We are home again!'

Then off they flew to find the old barn where each year the swallows built their nest, and the old farmhouse against which the house martins liked to put their homes of mud. It was lovely to be home again after being away all the long winter. Now sunny days, clouds of insects to eat, the joys of nesting and bringing up young ones lay before them, and the little birds were happy.

The creatures of the hedgerow did not very often speak to the flying swallows and martins, because, unlike other birds, they seldom perched on trees or bushes. All day long they flew in the air, and the rabbits grew used to their musical voices, twittering from dawn to dusk.

When they were making their nests the two lizards who lived on the bank near the pond watched the pretty little birds in surprise – for both swallows and martins came down to the pond side and scraped up mud in their beaks! The lizards thought at first that they were eating the mud, and wondered if there were insects in it.

'Why do you eat mud?' asked one lizard. 'It has no taste.'

The swallow could not answer because her beak was full of mud – but another swallow, who had just flown down to the pond side, answered the lizard.

'We are not eating mud!' she said with a twittering, laughing sound. 'We are taking it to build our nests.'

'But nests are not built of mud,' said the lizard, who had seen a robin building her nest in the hedgerow bank the year before, and thought he knew all about nests. 'They are built of roots, leaves and moss.'

'Not ours!' said the swallow. 'We make a saucer of mud on one of the beams of the old barn, and there we put our eggs, pretty white things with brown spots.'

'But doesn't the mud make your eggs dirty and wet?' asked the lizard.

'Of course not,' cried the swallow, thinking that the lizard must be very stupid. 'It dries hard and makes a fine nest. See, I will put a beakful of mud by your hole on the bank. You will see that it gets quite hard when it dries.'

The swallow dropped some mud in a tiny pile

beside the lizard's hole and then went back to the pond side again, scooping up some more mud in her beak. Then off she flew to the barn away across the field to dab the mud against the growing saucer nest she was building.

The martins came to the pond as often as the swallows, and the lizards grew to know them well while they were nest-building. But as soon as the nests were finished the twittering birds came no more to the pond side, but flew high in the blue summer sky all the day. Once or twice they saw the little lizards and called to them, but it was not until October came, with its chilly mornings and evenings, that the lizards saw the swallows to talk to once again.

Then they noticed that the telegraph wires that ran over the hedgerow, held up by a tall black pole, were quite weighted down with swallows and martins each evening. They seemed to be collecting together from all the fields around. The lizards looked at them in wonder. They could see the swallows with their steel-blue backs, long forked tails and chestnut-coloured throats, and they knew that the other birds, with shorter tails and a white patch at the lower end of their backs, were the little house martins.

Why were they all crowding together like this?

'*Feetafeetit, feetafeetit!*' cried the swallows gaily. 'It is time to go!'

'Where to?' asked the lizards, calling out to a swallow that skimmed low over the pond, trying to catch a fly.

'To a warmer land!' said the swallow. 'Come with us!'

'How far is it?' asked the lizard.

'Hundreds, thousands of miles!' cried the swallow. 'We fly with the north wind. We must go!'

'But why must you go?' asked the lizard. 'Don't go, swallow! We like to hear your twittering.'

'We are going to a land where there are plenty of insects,' said the swallow. 'If we stay here for the cold days, we should die of hunger.'

'No, you wouldn't,' said the lizard. 'The robin stays, and the thrush and blackbird, and they feed on insects. *I* feed on insects too.'

'Ah, but *you* go to sleep in the winter!' said the swallow. 'I know you do, because one spring we came back early and the lizards were still asleep in their holes, the lazy creatures! But we *must* go, lizard – I don't really know why we have to go, and I don't know the way – but when this time of year comes and the north wind begins to blow, something stirs inside me, and I feel I must fly to the south for miles upon miles!'

'It is a great adventure,' said the lizard.

'The greatest adventure in the world!' answered the swallow. 'We fly together in a big flock over the sea and over the land, over mountains and rivers, fields and forests. And all the time we cry to one another, for we are afraid of getting lost, especially at night or in a fog.'

'What if a storm comes?' asked the lizard, trembling

as he remembered a great storm that had happened in the summer.

'Ah, then we may perish!' said the swallow. 'But most of us get to the lands in the south, where the sun shines all day. We love it, but it isn't our home. We don't nest there. It is just a holiday for us, that's all! We shall all be longing for the spring to come again, for then one day we shall feel homesick for the fields and hills around here, and when the south wind blows to help us, we shall go with it – back to the old barns we love so well! I shall come back to my barn, and I will call to you as I dart over the hedgerow. Then you will know I have come back. You are sure you won't come with us?'

'How can I?' said the lizard impatiently. 'I have no wings. Besides, I should be afraid. I am not used to adventuring as you are.'

'Then goodbye!' called the swallow, and flew up to join his brothers and sisters on the telegraph wires. The lizard heard him excitedly twittering as he told all that had been said. The other birds twittered back, and the evening air was full of their sweet, high voices.

'Thank goodness they're going!' said a robin suddenly, looking out of the hedgerow. 'They eat too many insects. Food will soon get scarce. I should drive away those swallows if they stayed round here!'

'Don't get in a temper!' cried the swallows, hearing his high, creamy trill. 'We are going tonight, tonight, tonight!'

'The north wind is blowing!' twittered the martins. 'The sky is clear. It is time to go. We need not fly all the way at once. We can rest whenever we find good feeding grounds, for the wind is behind us. Let us go tonight, tonight, tonight!'

The rabbits came out to watch, and the hare stood upright in the nearby field. The hedgehog and her young ones felt the excitement too. The two lizards peeped trembling from their hole. The feathered adventurers were going on their long journey! All the animals longed to share in it.

Suddenly, in their hundreds, the swallows flew into the evening air, circled round once or twice, and then, in a great cloud, flew towards the south. '*Feetafeetit, feetafeetit!*' they called. 'Goodbye, goodbye! We will come back in the spring.'

They were gone. Soon not even the soft noise of their thousand wings could be heard. All the hedgerow creatures sighed and went back to their holes. They would miss the swallows and their bright voices – but the spring would bring them back again. Ah, but the spring was far away!

What adventurers! thought the rabbit, scuttling down her hole. *What daring little adventurers!*

The Crab with a
Long Tail

The Crab with a
Long Tail

IN THE big rock pool by the sea lived many creatures. There were crabs, big and little. There were little grey shrimps, and much bigger prawns. There were sea anemones, waving their feelers about, trying to catch their dinner.

It was an exciting place to live in, because the tide came in and out so often, bringing all kinds of treasures with it. Sometimes it was odd bits of seaweed that had floated in from deeper water. Sometimes it was empty shells. Sometimes it was a jellyfish or a starfish, who had tales to tell of the life they had led outside the big pool.

It was difficult to get out of the pool once any creature was in it. High rocks were set all around, and once you were there, you had to stay. So the creatures came to know one another very well indeed.

The big prawns darted backwards about the pool, using their strong tails to jerk themselves along. When they wanted to swim forwards, they used their little swimmerets, set under their tails. The shrimps darted about too, and if they wanted to hide from any enemy, they burrowed a little way into the sand so that they could not be seen.

The sea anemones sat close together on the rocks, looking like red or green lumps of jelly. Then suddenly they would open, unfurl their ring of feelers, and wave them about like thick petals. If any tiny water creature came near, the petals would close over him, and down he would go into the anemone's middle. That was the end of him.

The crabs all knew one another well. There were a few big crabs, some middle-size, and some quite small.

At times they had to go and hide themselves away in dark corners, where nobody would find them.

A big prawn was always surprised at this. He spoke to a shrimp.

'Where has that big green crab gone? He was rushing about the pool yesterday, staring at me with his eyes on stalks. I wanted to tell him something and now I can't find him.'

'I think I saw him going into that dark hole over there, under the rock,' said the shrimp. 'He didn't look very well.'

'It's most peculiar,' said the prawn. 'Crabs always seem to be going off into dark corners by themselves every now and then. What do they do there? Have they got a secret store of food?'

'I don't know,' said the shrimp. 'I don't like peeping at crabs too much. One gave me a nasty nip with his claws once, and I have never forgotten it.'

'Well, *I* shall go and see what that green crab is doing,' said the prawn. 'And if he has a secret store of food that he feasts on all by himself, I shall tell him what I think of him!'

So the prawn swam over to the dark hole and made his way inside, using his swimmerets to get him gently along. He kept his tail ready to jerk hard so that he could send himself quickly backwards out of the hole, if the crab was angry with him.

The crab was in the hole, right at the back, hidden by some seaweed. He took no notice of the prawn at all. He was behaving in a very strange manner.

He was wriggling about, turning and twisting himself from side to side as if he was in pain. Then he rubbed his horny legs hard against one another, making quite a noise. The prawn was alarmed.

'Are you ill?' he said. 'What is the matter, green crab? Why have you come here to do this?'

'Don't talk to me,' panted the crab. 'I am very, very busy. Go away.'

The prawn didn't go away. He stayed and watched the crab. The crab was so tired out that it lay quietly for a while, and then it began to wriggle about once more.

Suddenly the shell of the crab split right across its back! The prawn was amazed, and he backed away a little. Then the crab jumped right out of his old skin, and lay beside his shell. The split in the shell closed up, and the prawn stared in even greater surprise.

'I don't know which is you and which is your old shell,' said the prawn – and indeed, the two did look exactly the same, for the crab's shell was perfect, down to the smallest claw!

But the crab began to grow so fast that soon there was no doubt which was which! 'I feel better now,' he said. 'I shall grow quickly, and soon a new shell will begin to harden over my body. All crabs do this once a year till they are fully grown, prawn. You have no right to come and peep. Go away.'

The prawn went away to tell the exciting news to his friends. As he swam out into the pool, he saw a peculiar kind of creature. It would have been like a crab if it had not got a long tail!

'What are you?' asked the prawn, stopping to look. 'You look very much like a crab – but you have a long tail behind you. It looks a very soft tail too. You'd better be careful of it in case enemies come to eat it.'

'Oh dear, oh dear, I know that,' said the funny-looking crab, trying to tuck his tail under him. 'I did have a shell to tuck it into, but I've lost it. A big wave took me into this pool, and I am so afraid of meeting enemies everywhere.'

'There's a crab in that hole over there,' said the prawn. 'He's just jumped out of his shell, and he's feeling in quite a good temper now. Go and talk to him and see if he can help you.'

So the crab-with-a-long-tail went to talk to the green crab. 'I can't find a shell to put my tail into!' he wailed. 'What am I to do?'

'Well, you *are* a funny creature!' said the big crab. 'You wear armour as I do – except on your long tail.

My tail is fastened neatly beneath me. I do think it's silly of you to have such a long tail, if you can't grow a shell over it.'

'Oh, here's a shell to wear on it,' said the other crab. There was a small periwinkle shell in the hole, and he tucked his tail into it.

'That looks very silly,' said the big crab. 'Very silly indeed – like a little hat on your tail. What you want, crab, is a nice big empty whelk shell. If you could find one of those, you could first of all put your tail in, by crawling in backwards – then you could put all your body in – and you could guard the entrance to the shell by hanging out your claws.'

'That sounds such a good idea,' said the little crab, tucking his long tail under him again. 'If only I could find a whelk shell! But I'm so afraid that while I am looking for it someone will catch the end of my soft tail and nip it!'

'Well, I'm afraid I can't help you at the moment,' said the green crab. 'It will be a day or two before my own shell hardens over my body again. I daren't go out until then. But look – there's that prawn peeping in again. We'll make him help you.'

So they spoke to the prawn, who was only too glad to help, for he did love telling bits of news to all his friends.

'Do you know where there is a big empty whelk shell?' asked the crab. 'This friend of mine here, with a long tail, wants to make his home in one.'

'I'll find one for you, oh, I'll certainly find one for you!' said the prawn. He jerked his tail down and shot swiftly backwards, much to the small crab's surprise.

He was back again in two or three minutes. 'I've found just the thing!' he said. 'Come and see quickly, while there is no one about.'

The crab-with-a-long-tail followed the prawn, dragging himself along as quickly as he could. The prawn took him to where a big empty whelk shell lay on the sand. The crab was full of joy.

'It's fine!' he said. 'It's just the right size for me.

I'll put my tail into it straight away!'

He put his tail into it, right into the very end of the shell. He held on with a pair of little pincers he had at the tip of his tail. Then he pushed the rest of his body carefully into the shell. It really did fit him well.

He hung his big claws out of the entrance. 'Now no one can get me!' he said. 'My claws are guarding the only way in! When I want to walk about, I shall take my new home with me. I am so pleased. I shall always be your friend, prawn, and the friend of the other crab too!'

So, when the green crab had grown himself a fine new suit of armour and came out from his hole, the crab-with-a-long-tail (who was now called a hermit crab) and the prawn often met together for a meal. The hermit crab was good at finding food, and then you could see the three of them together enjoying it. The prawn always swam over their heads, picking up any bits of food that floated away.

You may often find a hermit crab on the seashore,

well tucked into an empty shell. Don't try to pull him out or you will hurt him. Wasn't it a good idea to tuck his tail into a shell?

The Little Ploughman

The Little Ploughman

JOHNNY WAS digging up his little garden. It was autumn, and all the gardeners were digging hard, so Johnny was doing the same.

Sometimes Johnny dug up a worm. He flew into quite a temper when he saw one. 'Horrid worm! What are you doing in my garden? I won't have you here!'

And then Johnny would drive his spade down on to the wriggling worm.

When his mother came out to see how he was getting on, she saw the poor worms, and she stared at them in surprise.

'Johnny! You surely haven't been killing the worms!'

'Yes, I have,' said Johnny. 'They're no use at all. They just wriggle about and make holes everywhere. I don't like them.'

'Johnny, we couldn't do without the worms,' said his mother. 'We really couldn't. They are like tiny ploughmen, working hard in the ground, day after day, night after night, all over the place.'

'Whatever do you mean, Mother?' said Johnny, surprised. 'Ploughmen! They haven't got ploughs! They don't turn up the earth, like ploughs do.'

'That's exactly what they *do* do!' said Mother. 'Look – come here on to our lawn, Johnny. Do you see these little mounds of earth, that we call worm casts? Well, those have been put there by the worms. It is earth from down below, that has been eaten by the worms, passed right through their bodies, and then thrown up to the grass.'

'Oh,' said Johnny. 'Yes, they do turn up the earth then – they do act like tiny ploughmen. Is that good, Mother?'

'Very good,' said his mother. 'It means that old, stale earth is always being brought up from below, and made into very fine powder at the top. Just feel a worm cast, Johnny, and see how fine it is.'

Johnny picked up a worm cast and crumbled it in his fingers. It was very fine indeed, like powder.

'I'm sorry I killed the worms now,' he said, looking rather red. 'I didn't think. I didn't know they were any use at all! I just thought they lived in their holes, and not doing a bit of good. Just stupid little creatures that the birds like to eat.'

'Oh, the worms aren't so stupid as you think,' said Mother. 'Come over here. Do you see these worm holes, all stuffed up with odds and ends?'

Johnny looked down at a worm hole. He could not see the opening, because someone had stuffed it up with dead leaves, stalks and bits of straw.

'Who put those things into the worm hole, and why did they do it?' he said in wonder.

'The worms did it,' said Mother. 'They like to keep

out the damp and the cold – so they carefully stuff up the entrance to their holes with anything handy. A clever idea, isn't it? They can't be so stupid as you thought, Johnny!'

'Does the worm live down its hole all the time?' asked Johnny.

'It has a kind of little room at the end of its hole,' said Mother. 'It lies there, coiled up. At night it comes out to feed. It may find a flower petal to eat, a bit of potato skin, or a dead leaf. If it finds nothing it likes, it simply eats the earth, for in the soil are tiny seeds and eggs. Then it throws the earth out, and makes those worm casts.'

'Well, I never knew worms were so interesting before,' said Johnny. 'You almost make me feel I'd like to keep some for pets, Mother!'

'Well, let's!' said his mother. 'We will make a wormery, Johnny, and the worms shall show you how they tunnel and plough for us! That will be a good idea.'

'Whatever is a wormery?' asked Johnny.

'Put down your spade, and we will make one together,' said his mother. So Johnny put down his spade and went with his mother. She went to the shed and took down an old glass jar. 'Go and wash it,' she said. So Johnny went and washed it well.

Then Mother said they were going to fill the jar. 'We will put five or six different layers in,' she said. 'Then you will be able to watch the worms mixing them all up, just as they mix up the earth for us below ground.'

Mother put a layer of ordinary soil into the jar, at the bottom. 'Now let's put some yellow sand out of my sandpit,' said Johnny.

So a layer of the yellow sand went in next. Then Johnny fetched some chalk, crushed it into powder, and put in a layer of that. That was three layers.

'Now what about a layer of gravel?' said Mother. 'And there is some fibre in that bag over there, that I use for planting my bulbs in – we'll put a layer of that too.'

'And here's some black charcoal,' said Johnny, getting quite excited. 'That's nice and black and will show up well, Mother. And let's put one last layer on the top – we can use earth again, can't we?'

'Right,' said his mother. They looked at the jar. It looked funny, with its seven different layers, all nice and even and straight.

'We must wet the layers,' said Mother, 'or the worms will not like their new home. They breathe through their bodies, you see, Johnny, so they do not like very dry earth.'

So they watered the layers well, and then they went to look for worms.

Johnny soon dug up three or four big ones. He put them on the top layer of the jar. By the time he had come back with another worm, all the others had disappeared!

'They must be down in the jar already,' said Johnny. 'Oh, yes – look – there's one tunnelling along the side of the glass, Mother. I can see it well. Look what a nice tunnel it has made!'

'We'll stand the jar on the windowsill in the nursery,' said Mother. 'Then we can watch each day and see how much work the worms do!'

So the jar was put on the windowsill. Johnny showed it to all his friends, and told them it was the wormery in which were his pet worms.

'You always said you didn't like the stupid worms and killed them,' said Peter in surprise.

'Well, they are not stupid, after all, and they do a lot of work for us underground, like little ploughmen, and I am not going to kill them any more!' said Johnny.

It was most surprising what the worms did in that big glass jar! By the very next day those straight layers had begun to go a little crooked!

'Look, Mother!' said Johnny. 'The layer of earth is mixing up with the layer of sand. And look – the fibre is mixing with the gravel.'

'So it is,' said Mother. 'The worms must have been

very busy!'

Day by day the worms tunnelled here and there in the layers. Day by day the layers went more and more crooked, and became mixed up with each other.

'Soon we shan't be able to tell one layer from another!' said Johnny.

He was quite right. After some time nobody could possibly tell how many layers had been put into the big jar, nor what they were! The jar just looked a real mixture of everything.

'It looks as if we took everything and mixed it up well before we put it into the jar!' said Johnny. 'No one would ever guess we had put those layers in so evenly and carefully.'

Johnny let his worms out after a while, and put them back into the earth.

'You are good little worms!' he said. 'Fine little ploughmen! You turn the earth up well for us, and mix it all up. You must be a great help to the farmers. I will never kill you again. Mother, I do wish all children knew how to make a wormery, and could keep one just to see what good little ploughmen the worms are! I wish somebody would tell them – then they could.'

Well, *I* have told you. So see if you can make one and watch your worms. You really will be surprised at what they do.

The Mistle
Thrush and the
Mistletoe

The Mistle Thrush and the Mistletoe

IN THE woods grew a tall holly tree. Its leaves were so prickly that no animal ever nibbled them. They were glossy and shiny, and the holly tree wore them all the year round.

Nearby was a big oak tree. It was green and thick all the summer, but in the winter its leaves had gone, and it stood bare and brown.

The holly tree was glad to keep its leaves. It did not like the look of the bare trees around. It thought it was a stupid idea to drop leaves in the autumn.

'Such a waste!' said the holly. 'Why bother to grow leaves just for a few months? I grow mine for years.'

'Don't you ever drop them?' asked the oak tree, bending its strong branches a little in the wind.

'Oh, yes, now and again,' said the holly tree. 'All evergreens drop their leaves now and again. You will find dry pine needles under the pine trees, and brown privet leaves under the privet bushes. And you will find dried-up holly leaves around my foot, if you cared to look! But I certainly don't throw my leaves away every winter.'

'You have some beautiful red berries on you,' said the oak tree. 'My acorns are all gone now. They have dropped off, as my leaves do. But you have your berries and your leaves too! You are very beautiful.'

'The children like to come and pick my sprays of shining leaves and scarlet berries to make their homes pretty at Christmas time,' said the holly. 'I am always proud of that.'

'I have something growing on me that the children come to pick too,' said the oak tree. 'But it does not really belong to me. It is a plant that grows on me and takes part of my sap for its food.'

'How strange!' said the holly. 'What is it?'

'It is a plant called mistletoe,' said the oak. Sure enough, growing from a stout branch of the oak, was a big green tuft of leaves, set with dim grey-green berries, like pearls.

Then the mistletoe spoke. 'Yes, I am the mistletoe. I cannot grow as you trees do, with proper roots in the ground. I have to grow on other trees, and get their help to grow my leaves and flowers and berries.'

'I don't like you,' said the oak. 'You are a robber plant. You steal from me!'

'I know,' said the mistletoe. 'But that is how I am made. I can't help it. I work with my leaves and get some of my own food from the sunlight and air – but as I have no proper roots, I have to get some of my food from you too, oak tree.'

'Each year you grow bigger and bigger,' grumbled the oak tree. 'If you get much bigger, you will rob me of too much sap, and then I shall feel ill and perhaps die.'

'I never grow very big,' said the mistletoe. 'I never grow bigger than a bush. Look – here are some children coming. Maybe they will pick me as well as the holly.'

'Oh look, look!' cried the children, as they came near the holly tree and the oak. 'Holly berries – and oh, mistletoe growing from the oak, as well! We can take some home for Christmas.'

So they cut some beautiful shining green sprays from the holly tree, set with bright red berries. Then they cut some sprays of the mistletoe, also set with berries, but not so bright or so beautiful as those of the holly.

The holly sprays were put round the pictures and looked gay against the walls. 'We do love the holly berries,' said the children.

The mistletoe was hung over the lamp, and over the doorway. 'It is to kiss one another under,' said the children. 'It is an old, old custom, isn't it, Mother, to kiss under the mistletoe?'

So, on Christmas morning, they kissed under the mistletoe, and wished each other a happy Christmas. The holly leaves shone in the firelight, and the mistletoe swung to and fro every time the door was opened.

'It's nice being here, isn't it?' said a holly spray to the mistletoe. 'It's fun when the children shout and laugh. I shall be sorry when Christmas is over and we are thrown away.'

'Thrown away!' said the mistletoe in dismay. 'Oh, we shan't be thrown away, shall we? I shan't like that.'

'Well, I shan't mind much,' said the holly. 'I expect I shall be thrown over the hedge into the field beyond – and some of my berries will lie in the ground and grow into tiny little holly trees. Perhaps the same thing will happen to you.'

'I don't want that to happen,' said the mistletoe. 'My berries will not grow in the ground. They will only grow if they are on the branches of trees.'

'How queer,' said the holly. 'Well, I'm afraid no one will throw you up into a tree! So your berries will be wasted.'

The holly was thrown over the hedge into the field, and its berries grew into tiny holly trees. But the mistletoe spray was put on the bird table.

'The mistle thrushes like the mistletoe berries,' said the children. 'So they shall have them.'

A big mistle thrush saw the spray of mistletoe and flew down at once. He pecked eagerly at the berries. They were very juicy, and the seeds inside were sticky.

'These berries are nice,' said the mistle thrush to the chaffinch. 'Leave them for me, please. I can eat them all.'

'You have some of the seeds stuck to your beak,' said the chaffinch. 'You do look funny!'

'Do I?' said the thrush. 'Well, I can wipe them off. Mistletoe berries are always sticky.'

He flew up to the branch of a nearby apple tree.

He wiped his beak there carefully. A seed fell off his beak and stuck to the branch.

The thrush flew away. The little seed rolled slowly down the side of the branch, sticking to it all the way. It came to the underside of the branch, and stayed there. It was happy because this was where it wanted to be.

'I should not grow in the ground,' said the seed to itself. 'I can only grow on the branch of a tree!'

It put out a funny little thing that pierced right through the bark of the apple branch. It was not a root. It was what is called a sinker, because it sank itself down into the tree.

The sinker reached the sap inside the tree. It fed on it. It took enough food from the apple tree to grow itself a pair of leaves.

When the mistle thrush sat in the apple tree he noticed the tiny mistletoe plant.

'How did *you* get here?' he sang.

'You planted me!' said the little mistletoe.

'I did not!' said the mistle thrush. 'I don't plant seeds!'

'But you planted *me*!' said the mistletoe. 'You cleaned your beak on this branch and left behind a seed. And I am that seed, grown into a little plant. I sent down sinkers into the branch, and I shall go on sending more and more, until I have grown into a great tuft of mistletoe!'

'How strange!' said the mistle thrush. 'And I suppose you too will have flowers and berries in good time – and I shall come along and feast on your berries, wipe the seeds away from my beak and start yet more mistletoe plants growing!'

'I will make my seeds very sticky, so that they will cling to your beak!' said the mistletoe.

'You are very clever,' said the thrush, and flew off on his quick wings.

The children noticed the mistletoe plant growing from their apple tree one day. 'Oh, look!' they cried. 'Here is a mistletoe bush growing out of the branch of an apple tree! How queer! Who could have planted it there? *We* didn't!'

'I did, I did, I did!' sang the big mistle thrush from a nearby tree. 'I planted it there with my beak! Yes, I wiped off the sticky seeds and left them there on the branch. And they grew, they grew. I planted the mistletoe, I did, I did, I did!'

The children heard him in surprise. 'Do you think he really did?' they said to one another. 'After all, he is called the *mistle* thrush – so perhaps he did!'

He certainly did. But you can plant a mistletoe seed too, if you want to! Just press it into a creak of the bark, and watch to see the mistletoe grow!

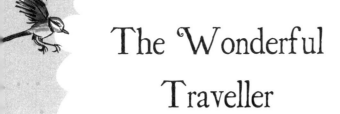

The Wonderful
Traveller

The Wonderful Traveller

IN THE pond that lay by the alder trees lived a long, strange creature, greenish-brown in colour, with a sharp snout and large eyes. It was a big eel, wise and much travelled, clever at hiding itself in the mud, and sharp at catching unwary fish or newts. Summer and winter it lived in the pond, sometimes leaving it to go for a short journey along the bottom of the ditch when it was muddy and wet. At the sight of the long, thick creature wriggling along, the frogs and toads froze with terror, for it was seldom that they saw the eel in their ditch.

The old toad who had lived under the hedgerow and spawned in the pond for many years knew the eel better than any other creature knew him. He had seen him come to the pond years before! The old toad had seen many strange things and watched scores of curious happenings with his bright coppery eyes. He was the oldest of all the hedgerow creatures, older even than the badger who sometimes came sniffing along the hedge on a warm night. He often sat and remembered all he had seen and heard, his eyes closed and his body squat, looking for all the world like a lump of earth!

It was while the toad was in the pond with his mate that he saw the eel again. First he saw a mist of mud rise up in the water near a big stone at the bottom. The toad knew that this meant some creature was under the stone, and he swam hurriedly to another stone he knew, and crept under it with his mate. As he watched from his hiding place he saw the eel wriggle out from under his big stone and dart at an unwary frog.

A little water vole, whose home had an entrance under the water not far from the toad's hiding place, called out to the toad, 'That's the end of that frog! He was always foolish! He was nearly eaten last week by the duck, and yesterday the heron nearly caught him. Now he is quite gone.'

'Only the strongest or wisest of us live a long life,' said the toad, blinking his eyes. 'I am very old.'

'Are you older than the eel?' asked the water vole.

'I was here when he came,' said the toad. 'But he was different then. He was much smaller, and his snout was broad, not sharp. His eyes were smaller too. He was not nearly so long as he is now, nor so thick in the body – but that was six years ago! I have watched him change and grow. He came here one spring morning. I remember it quite well.'

'Tell me about it,' begged the little water vole, who dearly loved a good story.

'I had finished spawning that year,' said the toad, shutting his eyes and trying to remember everything. 'I was squatting on the hedge bank in a rain shower, enjoying the drops on my back, not far from my stone there. I suddenly heard a strange noise in the ditch below.'

'What was it?' asked the water vole.

'I looked down,' said the toad. 'It wasn't a shuffling hedgehog. It wasn't a leaping frog. It wasn't a sliding snake. It was – the eel!'

'Where had he come from?' asked the water vole in surprise.

'I don't know,' said the toad. 'He just appeared from somewhere. He wriggled along the damp ditch and I followed him on the bank above, for I had never seen an eel before. He came at last to the pond and slid into it. He was only a little creature then, thin and half transparent. But, as you see, he has grown long and strong, and is an enemy to all small creatures who live in or near the water. He has never found a wife, and has never laid any eggs or had young ones. He is a strange, lonely creature.'

The eel swam up to the toad's stone, and at once the water vole disappeared into his hole in a great hurry. The toad did not move. He knew that the eel could not reach him, so he sat and looked at the long creature, marvelling at his great length.

'I heard what you said to the vole,' said the eel. 'You do not know everything, old toad. You are right when you say that I am a strange creature, but even you, wise though you are, could not even begin to guess the strange and wonderful life I have led, the long journeys I have made, and the long travels I have still to make! You are an old stay-at-home – I have travelled half across the world, and I shall do so again!'

The toad did not believe the eel.

'You are a boaster,' he said. 'You are like the frogs. They say they have been to the moon and back when they see it shining in a puddle!'

The eel was angry. It lashed its long tail and made little waves on the top of the pond.

'Listen to me,' it said. 'I was born thousands of miles away in the depths of an ocean.'

'What is an ocean?' asked the toad in surprise. 'Is it like this pond?'

'It is endless water!' said the eel. 'It is deep, so deep, and there are thousands of weird and marvellous creatures living in its depths, besides many beautiful fish. I have seen them all. I hatched out of an egg nine years ago, so I am old, very old. I was a strange-looking creature then, and knew little.'

'What were you like?' asked the toad curiously.

'I was leaf-like in shape,' said the eel, trying to remember, 'and very thin – as thin as that sheet of brown paper that once lay by the pond side. I am as long and round as a pipe now, I know, but in those days I was flat and you could have seen right through me, for I was transparent. I swam about for a while in the deep ocean and then I and many many thousands of other silvery eels began to swim to the north-east – and after about three years I came to land! I had changed on the way. I became smaller, and my body lost its shape and became rounder as it is now.'

'What did you do next?' asked the toad, his eyes nearly bulging out of his head with wonder at this strange story.

'I left the salt seawater and swam up a big river,' said the eel. 'Many companions were with me. We swam up in a great shoal. Then gradually our company broke up. Some entered small streams. Some swam to a lake. I found the ditch out there by the hedgerow. It was full of water then from the spring rains, and it led me to this pond. Here I have been ever since, growing bigger and longer each year. Ah, you should have seen me in that long journey, toad! Once we came to a lock gate, and it was shut – so we scrambled over it! And another time we came to a rushing waterfall, which, every time we tried to clamber up, knocked us down again. So we wriggled our way up the old moss-grown stones by the side of the waterfall. It was a great adventure.'

'Shall you stay here always?' asked the toad. 'What will happen if you grow bigger and bigger and bigger?

The pond will not hold you!'

'The time is nearly come when I must go again,' said the eel. 'I felt last December that I must go, for the ditches then were moist and easy to journey through, and the streams were full and rushed to the sea – so I started out, but I was caught in an eel trap and hurt my back. Then I came back here again to my pond to get better. But now I must soon go, for I have lost my greenish-brown colouring and have become silvery. All eels must go back to the salt sea when they become old. They must find wives and must lay their eggs in the deep ocean so that there may be thousands of other young eels to follow them. It will take me many months to reach my birthplace and I must go before I die.'

'Well, your tale is wonderful,' said the toad, his throat swelling with a loud croak. 'But I shall not be sorry to say goodbye to you, eel, for you have many a time tried to catch me, and you must have eaten hundreds of us in your life.'

'I would not eat a wise old toad like you,' promised the eel.

'You might not know it was I until you had swallowed me,' said the toad wisely, quite determined not to move from his safe hiding place.

Suddenly the eel twisted his head round and stared in amazement at a small creature which had just wriggled up to him. The toad stretched out his head to have a look. He saw another eel – but very, very small indeed.

'Where do you come from?' cried the large eel in delight and amazement.

'From the deep seas,' answered the small creature, who was so transparent that he looked as if he might almost be made of glass. 'I was born there, as you were, cousin. It has taken me three years and more to get to this pond. Is there good hunting here?'

'Plenty of everything,' answered the eel, swimming round his small cousin in delight. 'See how I have grown on the fare here. I am surely the biggest eel you have met in your journeys.'

'Oh, I have met far bigger eels than you,' said the small eel. 'Why did you not leave your pond earlier, cousin? You are old, and you should not leave your last long journey till you are weak, for it is a very long way. You may die before you get to our birthplace.'

'I shall go this very day,' said the big eel. 'Most of the old eels went in the autumn, I know, but we have had much rain lately, and the streams are full of water. It will be easy for me to swim down with the current, and I shall soon reach the sea.'

'Beware of eel traps, cousin,' warned the small eel. 'We elvers escaped them, for we are very small – but you are big.'

The eel called goodbye to the little elver and swam to the ditch that led into the pond. He wriggled into it and saw the old toad sitting high up on the bank, watching.

'Goodbye!' cried the eel. 'I go on my long journey back to the depths of the ocean again.'

'You are a wonderful traveller!' called back the toad. 'Goodbye! It is a pity you cannot take your small cousin with you. He will be just as much danger to us when he grows, as *you* have been. Goodbye – and good riddance!'

But the eel did not hear. He had left the pond and the hedgerow behind him for ever.

New Tails for Old

New Tails for Old

THE LITTLE pond that lay quietly by the old hedgerow had a few yellow leaves on its surface one early October morning. Autumn was coming, and the mornings and evenings were chilly. The water in the pond was not so warm now as it had been in the summer, and September's rain had filled it well, so that it was quite deep in the middle.

There was a warm, sandy patch on the bank near the pond, and on this sunny spot two small lizards liked to lie. They had lived there for a long time, for the hedgerow was undisturbed by humans, and not many of their enemies came along in the daytime.

In the pond below lived a friend of theirs, a smooth newt, a creature very like themselves in shape; they often talked to him and heard the pond news, and in return told him the news of the hedgerow.

They had seen him in the water one day, swimming to and fro. As they watched him they saw him rubbing his mouth and nose as if something hurt him there. He used his small front feet like hands, and it seemed to the watching lizards as if he were trying to undo the skin round his mouth. It was ragged there, and looked as if it were peeling off.

Suddenly all the skin on the newt's head became loose and at once the little creature began to wriggle about violently. Then the skin on his back loosened. It was a strange thing to see. The newt tried to take his feet out of the loose skin, but he could not. So he climbed out of the water and rubbed himself against a stone to loosen the skin. It was then that he saw the watching lizards, their eyelids blinking every now and again. For a moment the newt looked as if he were going to plunge back into the pond, but one of the lizards, the bigger one of the two, spoke to him.

'You are casting your skin,' he said. 'We do that too, but only in patches, not our whole skin at once as you are doing. Rub harder against the stone, newt – your skin will soon peel off altogether.'

The newt rubbed himself hard, and to his delight the skin became so loose that he was able to take his front legs out of their old skin covering. He slid down into the pond, wriggled again and at last swam right out of his old skin, leaving it floating in the water behind him, like a little ghost of himself. He felt better then, and once more climbed out upon the sunny bank to talk to the little lizards.

That was the beginning of their friendship. The lizards were bigger than the four-inch-long newt, and their skins were different, for their bodies were covered with small scales, like those on the bodies of snakes. The newt had a smooth skin, like a frog. He was olive brown on his back, but underneath he was a pretty orange colour, spotted with black. He proudly showed the lizards his lovely orange undersurface, but they at once raised themselves up and showed him that they too had a glowing orange colour on their underside.

'We are alike in many things,' said the lizards. 'We should be friends. Tell us, newt, why do you like the water so much? *We* would not swim in it no matter how warm it was.'

'Well, I was born in the water,' said the newt. 'I was one of five or six eggs laid against the leaf of a water plant. My mother folded the leaf over so that the eggs could not be seen. I hatched out into a tadpole.'

'A tadpole!' said the bigger lizard. 'But tadpoles grow into frogs!'

'Not always,' said the newt. 'Sometimes they grow into toads, and sometimes, if the eggs are laid by a newt, they grow into newts! I grew into a long fish-like tadpole. I expect you must have seen me swimming about in the pond when I was as small as that. But when the frog tadpoles lost their tails, I kept mine, because it is so useful in swimming.'

'Ah,' said the smaller lizard. 'You were wise to keep your tail. Tails are useful things. You never know what help your tail will be to you.'

'But what help is *your* tail?' asked the newt in surprise.

'Sh!' said one of the lizards quickly, as a buzzing noise was heard. 'Don't move. There are some bluebottle flies coming. They make a very tasty meal.'

All three were quiet, and soon four large bluebottles flew down and settled on the warm bank. With one swift movement the two lizards and the newt caught a bluebottle each, and the fourth fly shot away in panic.

'Very nice,' said the newt, swallowing. 'All kinds of flies are good.'

'And slugs too, and spiders,' said the bigger lizard. 'I remember once catching a—'

But what he was going to say the newt never knew, for suddenly there came a dark shape from the shadow of the hedgerow, and the terrified newt, glancing upwards, caught sight of sharp bared teeth.

'Rat!' he cried, slipping under a stone. 'Rat! Beware!'

One of the lizards, the smaller one, slipped under the stone with him, trembling with fright. But where was the big lizard? The two under the stone peeped out in fear, wondering if their companion had been eaten.

They saw a strange sight. The rat had pounced on the big lizard and had got him by the tapering tail. But, even as the two watchers looked on in horror, they saw the tail break off neatly, just as if it were made of brittle glass – and the lizard, tail-less but safe, glided to cover in a thick clump of grass. The rat made as if he would go after the escaping lizard, but he could not help watching the strange behaviour of the tail. It was jumping about as if it were alive! The rat at once put his paw on it, and forgot all about the lizard. In a trice he had eaten the wriggling tail, and then ran off into the hedgerow.

After a long while the lizard and the newt crept out once more into the sunshine – and to their joy they were joined by the other lizard too, looking rather queer and short because of his lost tail.

'It will grow again!' he said to the newt. 'That is just a good lizard trick. If an enemy catches me, I break off my tail, and leave it jumping about to attract his attention while I safely escape. I shan't have such a *nice* tail for my second one, but still, I'm alive, and that's all I care about. Didn't I tell you that tails were useful, newt?'

'You did,' said the newt. 'Well, I hope mine will be as useful to *me*! Now I am going back to the pond for a swim, so goodbye.'

All this had happened in the summertime and now it was autumn. The lizards were finding the mornings very cold, and they came out later and later. They had a very cosy hole under a big stone, and here they had decided to sleep for the winter, when they could find no flies to eat and were too cold to go hunting for spiders.

'I wish the newt would come and join us,' said the big lizard, blinking his eyelids sleepily in the October sunshine. 'We should sleep well together, the three of us, all our tails curled round one another.'

'Your new tail has grown well,' said the smaller lizard. 'It isn't so long as the other, but it does quite well. Look! There is the newt swimming just below us in the pond. Call him.'

But before the lizards could do anything to attract the newt's attention there came the loud flap-flap-flap of large wings, and a great heron flew slowly down to the pond. It stood on its long legs not far from the lizards, who at once fled under their stone. Then the big bird put its head on one side and watched for a fish or a frog, for it was hungry on this cold October morning.

The newt had been busy eating a water grub and had not noticed the heron. All he saw now was what looked like two great sticks of yellow in the water –

the legs of the waiting heron, although the newt did not know it. The little creature swam about below, little guessing that the big heron, with its long strong beak, was watching his every movement out of sharp and hungry eyes. Suddenly the heron flashed its long beak into the water, trying to spear the newt – but just in time the frightened animal darted off, only to find that the heron, instead of stabbing him through the body, had got him by the tail!

He wriggled manfully as the heron lifted up his head to take him from the water and swallow him whole – and in a trice he remembered how the lizard had escaped from the rat by breaking off his tail. Quickly the newt did the same, dropping back safely into the water, leaving his poor little tail in the beak of the disappointed heron. He was saved – but how queer it was to swim through the water without a tail! He could not get along.

He hid under a stone in the water until the heron had flown off. Then awkwardly he clambered up the bank to where his two lizard friends awaited him.

'Tails *are* useful,' he told them. 'I hope mine will grow in time for the spring. But now it is autumn and if you will have me, I will hide with you under your stone to sleep for the wintertime.'

Then all three curled up close together, their little feet holding tightly to one another, and there they sleep soundly in the safety of their stone shelter under the old hedgerow. Not even the rat guesses where they are.

Acknowledgements

All efforts have been made to seek necessary permissions. The stories in this publication first appeared in the following publications:

'The Little Fawn' first appeared in *The Teachers World*, No. 1676, 1935.

'The Wonderful Carpet' first appeared in *The Enid Blyton Nature Readers*, No. 13, Macmillan, 1945.

'Dozymouse and Flittermouse' first appeared in *The Teachers World*, No. 1640, 1935.

'The Poor Little Sparrow' first appeared in *Enid Blyton's Sunny Stories*, No. 112, 1939.

'The Sunset Fairies' first appeared in *The Teachers World*, No. 1159, 1926.

'The Grey Miner' first appeared in *The Teachers World*, No. 1644, 1934.

NATURE STORIES

'The Pixies and the Primrose' first appeared in *The Teachers World*, No. 1770, 1937.

'How Derry the Dormouse Lost his Secret' first appeared in *Sunny Stories for Little Folks*, No. 62, 1929.

'The Blue Visitor' first appeared in *The Teachers World*, No. 1672, 1935.

'The Tail of Bup the Bunny' first appeared in *Sunny Stories for Little Folks*, No. 85, 1930.

'The Funny Little Hedgehog' first appeared in *Enid Blyton's Sunny Stories*, No. 77, 1938.

'Susan and the Birds' first appeared in *The Enid Blyton Nature Readers*, No. 29, Macmillan, 1946.

'The Ugly Old Toad' first appeared in *Enid Blyton's Sunny Stories*, No. 354, 1945.

'Belinda and the Bulbs' first appeared in *Sunny Stories for Little Folks*, No. 132, 1931.

'Sly the Squirrel Gets a Shock' first appeared in *Enid Blyton's Sunny Stories*, No. 311, 1943.

'Lightwing the Swallow' first appeared in *The Teachers World*, No. 1844, 1938.

ACKNOWLEDGEMENTS

'The Elm Tree and the Willow' first appeared as 'The Elm-Tree and the Willow' in *The Teachers World*, No. 1691, 1935.

'Black Bibs' first appeared in *The Teachers World*, No. 1703, 1936.

'Where Shall We Nest?' first appeared in *Enid Blyton Nature Readers*, No. 3, Macmillan, 1945.

'Betty and the Lambs' Tails' first appeared in *Enid Blyton Nature Readers*, No. 4, Macmillan, 1945.

'The Cross Little Tadpole' first appeared in *Enid Blyton Nature Readers*, No. 5, Macmillan, 1945.

'The Bumblebee Hums' first appeared as 'The Bumble-Bee Hums' in *The Teachers World*, No. 1670, 1935.

'Rabbity Ways' first appeared in *The Teachers World*, No. 1632, 1934.

'The Whistler' first appeared in *The Teachers World*, No. 1666, 1935.

'The Adventurers' first appeared in *The Teachers World*, No. 1638, 1934.

NATURE STORIES

'The Crab with a Long Tail' first appeared in *Enid Blyton Nature Readers*, No. 19, Macmillan, 1945.

'The Little Ploughman' first appeared in *Enid Blyton Nature Readers*, No. 26, 1946.

'The Mistle Thrush and the Mistletoe' first appeared as 'The Mistle-thrush and the Mistletoe' in *Enid Blyton Nature Readers*, No. 28, Macmillan, 1946.

'The Wonderful Traveller' first appeared in *The Teachers World*, No. 1660, 1935.

'New Tails for Old' first appeared in *The Teachers World*, No. 1636, 1934.

Also available:

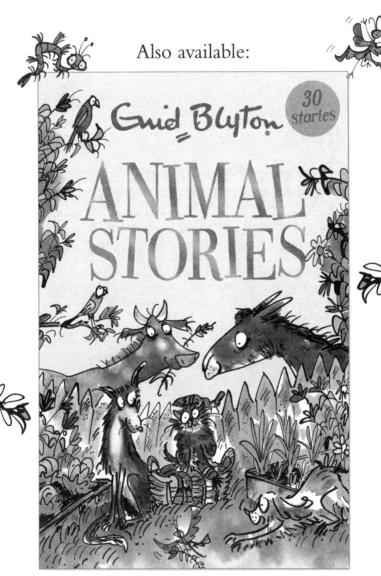

Enid Blyton

30 stories

ANIMAL STORIES

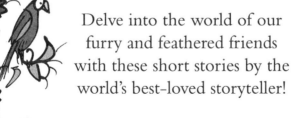

Delve into the world of our furry and feathered friends with these short stories by the world's best-loved storyteller!

Also available:

Enid Blyton

SPRINGTIME STORIES

30 stories

Head off on sparkling springtime adventures with these short stories by the world's best-loved storyteller!

ENIDBLYTON.CO.UK
IS FOR PARENTS, CHILDREN AND TEACHERS!

Sign up to the newsletter on the homepage for a monthly round-up of news from the world of

JOIN US ON SOCIAL MEDIA

Enid Blyton

is one of the most popular children's authors of all time. Her books have sold over 500 million copies and have been translated into other languages more often than any other children's author.

Enid Blyton adored writing for children. She wrote over 700 books and about 2,000 short stories. *The Famous Five* books, now 75 years old, are her most popular. She is also the author of other favourites including *The Secret Seven*, *The Magic Faraway Tree*, *Malory Towers* and *Noddy*.

Born in London in 1897, Enid lived much of her life in Buckinghamshire and loved dogs, gardening and the countryside. She was very knowledgeable about trees, flowers, birds and animals. Dorset – where some of the Famous Five's adventures are set – was a favourite place of hers too.

Enid Blyton's stories are read and loved by millions of children (and grown-ups) all over the world. Visit enidblyton.co.uk to discover more.